DAPHNE FEARED HIM ... HATED HIM ... AND LOVED HIM MORE THAN HER HEART COULD BEAR ...

Panic gripped the crowd as acrid smoke billowed forth from the flaming building. The fire took only seconds to spread through the building. People screamed, pushing against one another, desperate to get away from the blaze. Daphne began to choke as she inhaled smoke.

She caught sight of a dark head far away from her and her heart lurched.

"Rene!" she shouted through parched lips.

The man did not move or respond. Daphne's head drooped in sorrow. She had been mistaken once more.

"Daphne!" His response broke through the bellowing noise of the crowd.

He was alive! Daphne was flooded with inexpressible joy. She stretched one hand forward to try to reach him and they struggled toward one another. But the surging crowd came between them.

Suddenly, Rene saw a large, heavyset man move purposely toward Daphne, tipping a small vial into a handkerchief. Rene struggled feverishly to reach Daphne before the stranger did. He yelled in fury. Too late! Without warning, the thug grabbed Daphne from behind and pressed a chloroform-soaked handkerchief to her face. She slumped into his arms.

Rene clawed at the people who separated him from Daphne. There was nothing he could do. He was trapped by the crowd. It was like some dreadful nightmare, only worse ...

A Destiny of Love

A Destiny of Love

Ivy St. David

Exclusive Distribution
by
PARADISE PRESS, INC.

Published by:
Paradise Press, Inc.
12956 S.W. 133rd Court
Miami, FL 33186

Printed in the United States of America

TO MY GRANDPARENTS,
Michael and Gertrude Murphy Dupont
and
Albert and Helen Utano Loiacono

Chapter 1

reddish-blonde curls and urged Coral into a gallop. The wind rushed past Daphne's hot cheeks, jerking to

Pittsburgh, Pennsylvania—1877

"I won't marry him, no matter what Papa says," whispered Daphne Slater into her horse's ear. Coral shook her fine head.

"So you agree with me," laughed Daphne, her blue eyes bright. "You're a good girl, Coral."

Daphne quickly slipped again into the tragic mood that had made her rush out of the house and into the stables. The stormy breakfast with her aunt and father had left all the servants talking. Parsons, the old stableman, had saddled her roan mare, knowing that the only cure for Daphne's rampages was a brisk canter across the fields.

"Papa always said that I should marry for love, just as he and Mama did. Why must he push that odious Caleb Winters on me?" Daphne tossed her long reddish-blonde curls and urged Coral into a gallop. The wind rushed past Daphne's hot cheeks, jerking to

3

and fro the green feathers in her hat. Her full mouth turned up at the corners, forming an impish grin. For the first time since her quarrel with her father and Aunt Elspeth, Daphne smiled, enjoying the beautiful June morning.

"I'll get around Papa, Coral, you wait and see. Haven't I always been able to? He told me I couldn't have you, my darling, and didn't I bring him around? It's all Aunt Elspeth's fault. She's always after me to make a good match. I'll marry when I want to and whom I want to. Or maybe I won't marry at all. I'll go off to Africa and become a missionary nurse."

Here Daphne went off into one of her favorite daydreams, inspired by the visit of a handsome young missionary to her church. That her other favorite daydream involved her going to a glittering ball in some fabulous European capital and meeting a real prince who would fall instantly in love with her did not bother Daphne.

Daphne smiled as she imagined herself leading a small boy in his first prayers. Her lips moved as she instructed him, "Now I lay me down to sleep. . . ." Suddenly an enormous tiger ran into the tent. Daphne held the little boy out of the reach of the tiger's fangs. What should she do? A gun materialized in her hand and she shot the tiger dead.

"I don't know if I would really like being a missionary," Daphne shuddered. "I think I would much rather go to Vienna and meet a real prince."

The moonlight shone down into the ballroom, deserted except for the prince and Daphne. Waltz music floated in the air. The prince took her in his arms and they began dancing as though they were floating as well. Daphne's pink and silver gown glistened around her shoulders as the prince leaned down to. . . .

Coral whinnied. "So you're tired of walking are you, old girl? You'd like to run, would you?" Daphne urged on the spirited mare once again.

Coral cantered along as the country lane wound its way up the side of the hill. The sunlight shone down between the elms and beeches lining the road, dappling Coral's strawberry coat and bringing out the red highlights in Daphne's long, fair hair.

Daphne reined in the horse at Lookout Point and dismounted, leading Coral along by her halter. Lookout Point was Daphne's favorite place, chiefly because it overlooked her city. Pittsburgh was a-bustle with activity on this morning in the busiest and most enterprising city in the world. Why, Daphne reflected, almost everything you could think of was made here, everything important like steel and iron and tools. Thick smoke hung over the city in an enormous cloud and more went up in plumes from the huge ovens that cooked the pig iron and made it into steel. The valley was almost entirely covered by a grey haze. As the morning breezes wafted the smoke around, Daphne could make out the two rivers encircling the city. She could even see her father's barges bringing iron down from the richest fields in the world near Lake Superior.

Across the valley, in the hills, coal cars climbed up and down like so many ants, suddenly disappearing down mine shafts to bring up the coal hidden in the earth. Daphne could not make out the name on the side of the coal cars, but she knew what it was: Winterhaven Mines. Caleb owned the largest mines in Pittsburgh.

She was sick of hearing what a wonderful man Caleb was, of being told that it was her duty to marry him. Why couldn't her aunt and her father just leave her alone?

"Caleb is the most horrid man in the world, even if he is handsome and the richest man in town. Papa wants me to marry him so they can make better business deals. That's all. He practically admitted as much himself," concluded Daphne petulantly. Her pride had been hurt by Caleb's prosaic, unromantic proposal of marriage. She knew that Caleb didn't really love her. "Oh, Coral, whatever am I going to do? I can't marry Caleb. I can't. I don't love him and I never could! And he certainly doesn't love me."

Daphne threw herself against Coral's sleek neck and cried as though her heart would break. Her own dear father wanted her to do something that was hateful to her. Daphne couldn't bear it. She didn't want to disappoint her father, but she refused to give up her life for him.

"I'll run away from home and be a missionary. Really I will, Coral. Oh, but how can I leave you and all my pretty things and my home?"

Daphne probably would have cried all morning except that it was too lovely a day. A tiny goldfinch flew among the cherry blossoms of a nearby tree and Daphne stopped to watch the little bird build its nest.

"How can I be sad in this lovely world, Coral? I could never be a tragic heroine like the kind I read about in books. I haven't the disposition for it." Daphne sighed as piteously as any tragic heroine at the thought and liked the effect so much that she sighed again. Then she laughed, perhaps at herself or perhaps at the little gold bird so busily building its nest.

"Well, Coral, it's time for us to be going home. If I'm going to get out of marrying Caleb, I'll have to work at it. I'd better get started. You can catch more flies with honey, you know!"

Daphne led Coral over to the mounting bench and sprang up onto her back the way she had seen circus ladies do. It was something she had practiced for months, but could never show anyone. It wasn't ladylike, certainly not for a young woman of seventeen who had attended a seminary.

Feeling calmer, as she always did after a visit to Lookout Point, Daphne turned Coral's head toward home. She began to hum a tune she had heard at the Academy of Music the night before last. That was the evening Caleb had proposed to her, and she had rejected him.

Daphne was nearly home when she heard the sound of horses cantering toward her from behind. She reined Coral over to the side of the road to let the riders pass.

"Good morning, Miss Daphne," came the unmistakable deep voice of Caleb Winters.

"Why, Daphne, how lovely to see you," chimed in the high, dainty voice of Caleb's sister, Catherine.

Daphne turned. As usual, she was struck by the picture they presented. Caleb was a big, handsome, blond man with a florid complexion. He exuded good health and vitality, and was tremendously strong. His blue eyes sparkled and his beard glistened. Next to him, Catherine seemed pale and insignificant, as though her brother had drawn all the energy out of her. She had light hair and pale blue eyes surrounded by colorless lashes. But her face was delicately heart-shaped and she would have been pretty had she had any color.

It was Daphne's private opinion, shared by most of Pittsburgh, that Caleb had indeed taken all of Catherine's exuberance. He seemed to soak the life from everyone. All her life, Catherine had been bullied by Caleb. At seventeen, she was, of course, much younger than her thirty-four-year-old brother. Their father, Sebastian Winters, had died when Catherine was a baby, and Catherine treated Caleb as a father. Since they were best friends, Daphne had tried to tell Catherine that she needn't treat her brother as though he were her lord and master.

"Cat got your tongue, miss?" asked Caleb, startling Daphne out of her reverie.

"Pish-posh. Good day to you, Catherine, Caleb."

"It's a lovely morning for a ride, isn't it? But don't you think it's awfully dangerous riding out alone?" worried Catherine.

"Nonsense, Cath. What could happen here in Pittsburgh on a lovely summer's day?"

"What, indeed, Catherine. You should be more like Daphne. Less of a timid tabby. You know, Daphne, Catherine is still afraid of the dark."

"I am not, Caleb. It's only since Mama died . . ."

"There now, Cath," soothed Daphne, leaning over to pat her hand. "And where have you two been so early this fine June morning?"

"One might ask the same of you, miss."

"Oh, Coral likes a bit of a jaunt."

"And so does her mistress, if I don't mistake myself."

"Why, yes, on a fine morning," Daphne admitted,

coloring despite herself. Although she disliked Caleb, she did not want him to think her a hoyden.

"And it is a fine morning, is it not, Miss Daphne? I think you and I might profit by taking a ride together, alone."

"I'm afraid not, Mr. Winters. My aunt will be expecting me home shortly."

"I doubt that your aunt will be overly displeased if you are with me. I will beg her pardon myself."

"She will not be placated."

"Oh, but she will be."

"You are very sure of yourself, sir."

Catherine ventured timidly, "Caleb, you must let Daphne go home if she thinks it best."

"Mind your own business, sister," Caleb snarled. "Run along home. I'll join you for lunch. Daphne and I have matters to discuss which needn't trouble you."

"Yes, Caleb, if you think it's safe," acquiesced Catherine.

"If I didn't think it perfectly safe, I wouldn't tell you to do it, would I? Don't be a ninny, Catherine."

"No, brother, it is only that there are so many men around the streets standing idle and hungry."

"If they are hungry it is their own fault. There is work to be found if only those laggards would look for it. Run along home."

"If Catherine doesn't want to ride home alone, I'll accompany her. I'm not in the least afraid," interposed Daphne, hating to see Caleb treat his timid sister so cruelly.

"It doesn't suit me for you to accompany her. She can easily enough ride home alone. I'll have no more of this nonsense. Really, Catherine, you are most tiresome."

9

"I am sorry, Caleb," said Catherine with a trembling chin. "It was foolish of me to contradict you. Daphne, I believe we have an appointment at the dressmaker the day after tomorrow, don't we?"

"Yes, I'll meet you there. There really is no danger. Just spur your horse on."

"Good-bye, Catherine," Caleb said meaningfully.

"Good day to you both," replied Catherine, riding off reluctantly down the road.

"What is it you want with me, Mr. Winters, that compels you to force your company on me against my wishes?"

"You know very well what I want, but we shall discuss it privately. Come along."

Reluctantly, Daphne rode off with Caleb back toward Lookout Point, her mind no longer occupied with Catherine. Caleb drove all other thoughts from her mind. She would need all her wits to keep him at arm's length and to prevent him from repeating his proposal of marriage.

Daphne set her chin in a most determined manner, completely unaware that she presented a most appealing picture. Caleb longed to touch her soft, rosy cheeks, to run his fingertip down her small, straight nose, to taste her firm, full lips and to lose himself in those wonderful red-blonde curls. He clenched his reins in frustration. He would have her; she would be his at any cost. He was not a man to get the worst of any deal, whether he was buying a coal mine . . . or a wife!

Once again, Daphne found herself at Lookout Point, but this time under less pleasant circumstances. The city below her rested between the arms of the Allegheny and the Monongahela Rivers and was cradled by its encircling hills. The forges burned brightly, the noise of the machinery carried up the hill, coal cars clattered about, barges went downriver, but Daphne noticed none of it. She was preparing to fight Caleb for her happiness and her life. She refused to bend to his every whim as Catherine did.

Daphne and Caleb tethered their horses by the mounting block and walked toward the top of the hill.

"You know I want to marry you and yet you say no. Your father already has consented. Do you find me so hateful?" Caleb's eyes searched Daphne's. "I would be a good husband to you, Daphne. You and Catherine get along well and we could all live together at Winterhaven. I want you to be my wife. Must I go down on my knee before you like a lovesick schoolboy?"

Daphne stifled a giggle as the image rose in her mind. "Caleb, I never will marry you."

She cast wildly around for a way of convincing him and suddenly a wonderful idea occurred to her. "I am pledged to a higher purpose," she said softly, her eyes cast down modestly.

Had she been looking up, Daphne would have noted a puzzled and highly amused expression flit across Caleb's features. "What do you mean, Daphne?" he asked.

"I am resolved to devote my life to missionary work."

There was a pause and then Caleb said impatiently, "I can scarcely believe that."

"It is true. I'll be leaving for Africa shortly." She did not dare look up for fear of giving herself away.

"Indeed? Odd that your father didn't mention

this to me. Your living in Africa would indeed stand in the way of our marriage."

"I am so pleased that you understand," Daphne smiled, glancing quickly upward.

"No, I never suspected that you had such ambition, especially not after the way you so obviously enjoyed the program at the music hall the other night. And not after watching you gobble ice cream after the program."

"I did no such thing!" protested Daphne hotly. "Naturally, everyone enjoys culture. We who are planning to go into mission work, however, must give up certain things. But there are compensations."

"Naturally," responded Caleb gravely. "Tell me, when do you leave for Africa?"

"Oh, soon," answered Daphne airily, hoping that Caleb wouldn't ask her too many specific questions.

"And what part of Africa do you intend to serve in? It wouldn't by any chance be the country Reverend Entwhistle is serving in, would it?"

"Why, yes," replied Daphne eagerly, glad that he had answered his own question.

"Well, I do admire you. Rushing off to Africa just like that, Miss Daphne. I am sure that you'll make a superior missionary. But dear Daphne, I can't let you go. I am determined to follow you to Africa," Caleb declared.

"I believe you are mocking me, sir."

"And I believe you have been doing the same to me, my fine missionary. Now, in seriousness, tell me why you won't be my wife."

"I don't love you."

Caleb laughed shortly. "I fail to see how that enters into the matter. We will come to love one another all in good time. We are well suited, you know, Daphne."

"I do not think so."

"But your father does."

"Papa is not the one you are trying to marry. The salient point is that I don't think we are well suited."

"A young girl's duty is to obey her parents. After she is married, she must obey her husband."

"It is every person's duty to obey his or her conscience first. You have to understand that I don't love you and that I can marry only for love."

"You are a romantic child. But I don't doubt that you will soon see reason."

"You admit that you don't love me. Why do you want to marry me?"

"As I said before, we are compatible." Caleb looked at her meditatively. "Or will be, once you are grown."

"You great oaf!" responded Daphne, stung by the jibe. "I'll never marry you, no matter how old I become. You bully your sister and you would bully me if I were yours to command. The only reason you and Papa wish us to marry is to enhance your business interests."

"One day you will take back those words. Very well, business considerations do enter into my desire to marry you. But they are not all. We shall come to love one another in time. I feel great affection for you even now. I find you most charming and very beautiful, despite your unruly temper. Your Aunt Elspeth warned me that I'd find you intractable."

"I know my own mind and I see no need to be ashamed of that. I'll go now. I have given you my answer and my reasons. I will not marry you," said Daphne with great dignity as she turned away.

"I didn't give you permission to go," Caleb growled, gripping her arm and turning her to face him.

"I don't require your permission. Unhand me, sir."

Their eyes met and locked in combat. Daphne felt almost afraid of this big, powerful man she had known all her life. Caleb looked like some angry and dangerous animal ready to pounce.

"I said, let me go."

"I will have you, Daphne. I will." He pulled Daphne to him, forcing her face up, and brought his lips down on hers.

Fear gave Daphne more strength than she knew she possessed, and she kicked out at him.

"You vixen!" cried Caleb, rubbing his shins. Daphne hitched up her skirts and ran off. She mounted Coral quickly and kicked the startled mare into a fierce gallop.

"You will be mine. Just as the city is mine. You will be mine," Caleb muttered to himself as he watched her gallop away.

Chapter 2

Daphne rushed into the house and slammed the door. The stained-glass fan-light above it rattled. She swept up the stairs to the safety of her bedroom.

"Oh, Letty," cried Daphne to her maid, "the most awful thing has happened. But I don't think I can tell even you about it."

"What is it, Miss Daphne?" Letty asked in her soothing way.

Daphne poured out her story as Letty listened sympathetically.

"Oh, Daphne," Letty sighed. "Refusing to marry the man of your father's choice and kicking him and running about on horseback like a hooligan. I certainly didn't bring you up to act that way."

"No, Letty, you old dear, I brought myself up to act that way. You can't make a silk purse out of a sow's ear, you know," Daphne smiled, her spirits nearly restored. "Now that I've kicked him, perhaps he won't want to marry me."

Seeing no point in pursuing the matter, Letty handed Daphne a note. "This was brought round for you today."

"Thank you, Letty," said Daphne, taking the letter and sitting down in the little yellow chair by the window to read.

"It's from Tad. He must be home from the university."

The brief note read:

Daphne—I must talk to you. Meet me at the old secret place by the quarry at midnight.— Tad.

"What great fun! We haven't met out by the quarry since we were children. Perhaps I can make Tad run off and marry me." The thought of marrying Tad, her childhood friend, set Daphne into merry peals of laughter. Tad was a thin, serious boy. He had been rather sickly in childhood and still looked quite frail. With his thick glasses and pale skin, he hardly had seemed a likely playmate for the bouncing healthy Daphne.

But they had been the best of friends. His imagination had intrigued Daphne and together they had played fanciful games and invented secret places. The hollow trunk of the old oak tree near the quarry was one of their favorite places. Tad would sneak out and meet Daphne there on days when his mother had put him to bed saying he was too sick to go out and play. Daphne was still child enough to believe that the reason he wished to meet her at the old oak at midnight was to tell her of some new game he had invented for them to play.

As Daphne put on her new foulard dress with the modish bustle at the back and the leg-of-mutton sleeves, she considered how she ought to deal with her father and aunt. Aunt Elspeth, Daphne's father's sister, had lived with them since Daphne's mother had died when the child was only three. Elspeth Slater was a tall, bony spinster of forty-five with serious views on religion, drink and the conduct appropriate to a young lady. She was president of both the Ladies Christian Missionary Union and the Temperance League. She and Daphne had never gotten along well.

Daphne pulled her hairbrush through her long curls and then pulled them back from her face, holding them in place with tortoiseshell combs. She stood up and examined herself in the full-length mirror. The bright green of the dress suited her reddish-blonde hair and the black braiding at the wrists, waist, neck and shoulders set the gown off perfectly.

I'll act as though nothing has happened, she thought, and tonight I'll be extra nice to Papa and Aunt Elspeth.

Daphne entered the small salon where she and her aunt always waited for her father to come home from the office. "Good evening, Aunt," Daphne smiled as she leaned over and kissed Elspeth Slater's brow.

"Good evening, Daphne. I fear that you have been frightfully neglectful of your embroidery," lectured her aunt, her light blue eyes flickering disapproval. Her grey hair was pulled severely back and her skin was sallow—a drab face, enlivened only by the piercing blue eyes. As usual, Elspeth's own fingers were busily knitting socks for the poor in Africa. Daphne had always wondered what the Africans did with so many socks in that hot continent. When

Daphne had questioned her aunt about it, she had received not an answer, but a severe look.

"Yes, Aunt," replied Daphne, mindful of the need to win her aunt over. She picked up the hated embroidery and began to work at it. It read "A Lady Is As A Lady Does" and was intended to remind Daphne to improve her own decorum.

"You are working the stitches sloppily."

"Yes, Aunt."

"And don't fawn over me because I cannot abide that. What have you been up to today? You are only pleasant when you are trying to pull the wool over my eyes."

Daphne bit her lip to stop the angry words from flying out of her mouth. "I went for a ride this morning, Aunt. In the afternoon I read and worked in the garden."

"Always reading novels. What will you come to? And dashing about on that animal. I told your father not to buy it for you, but would he listen to me? No! I have raised you just as a mother would, yet my opinion counts for nothing."

"What's this, Elspeth?" asked Jeb Slater, entering the room suddenly. "Your opinion counts for a great deal and Daphne and I are most grateful to you, aren't we, my girl?"

"Indeed, Papa." Daphne hugged her father. He always seemed to smell of the river and tar, and of pipe smoke. Jeb Slater was not a tall man, but he seemed sure of himself. Having an almost military bearing, he could be quite imposing. His eyes were blue and his hair, once black, was now salt-and-pepper, as was his short beard. Jeb Slater was only forty-one, but he looked older.

"Ah, it's good to be home to peace and quiet after a long day by the river," he sighed.

Daphne was surprised to see deep circles under her father's eyes. What could he be worrying about? She flushed guiltily. Was it her refusal to marry Caleb? Jeb saw her staring at him and forced himself to brighten. He couldn't have her suspecting anything.

"Is that.lamb I smell, Elspeth? How nice! Shall we go in to dinner?"

The three of them entered the dining room and seated themselves at one end of the walnut dining table. Hawkins, the butler, brought in the roast immediately and began to carve, while Marie passed the mint jelly and the roast potatoes.

Daphne, determined to put her father in a good mood, maintained her most ladylike demeanor. "What did you do today, Papa? How many barges came down from the mines?" she asked cheerfully.

"Seven," answered her father, motioning to Hawkins for another helping of honeyed carrots.

"And did you get a good price for everything?"

"Why you little minx, I believe you could run my business better than I do. You have quite a good head for it. Well, prices are going up a bit. It's not the best of times, though. We are in the midst of a depression." Once again, Daphne noticed that Jeb looked worn and tired.

"Let your father eat in peace, Daphne. Don't be constantly plaguing him for attention. Men don't like that sort of behavior," Elspeth put in waspishly.

Daphne lowered her eyes and picked at her food.

"Nonsense, Elspeth, a little conversation at dinner is a fine thing and I like to hear Daphne prattling on.

But let's talk about something different. I've had enough of business."

Elspeth and Jeb discussed their plans for a party, and soon pecan pie was served.

"This has been a good dinner, Elspeth. And I'm glad we've had no more of your obstinacy, Daphne."

"No, Papa," replied Daphne meekly.

"So you've curbed your temper and are willing to listen to reason?" Daphne nodded. "Caleb Winters is as fine a man as any you'll find and I am pleased that you've decided to marry him."

"Oh, no, Papa! I never could do that!"

"What? I thought you had decided to be reasonable."

"I am being reasonable. It is you who are being unreasonable," objected Daphne before she could stop herself.

"You still maintain that you will not marry him?"

"Yes."

"And why is that?"

"I don't love him and I never could. Nor do I even like him. He is a brute and a bully."

"That is not so," interposed Elspeth. "Your father wouldn't allow you to marry someone who might treat you badly and you know that, Daphne. Caleb is merely a firm man. Like any man, he will demand obedience of his wife."

"I don't want to be obedient."

"What sort of childish nonsense is this, Daphne?" asked Jeb, growing more and more angry.

"My feelings are not nonsense. I don't like Caleb, not in the least. He is too old for me. And he doesn't love me, either." Daphne was close to tears.

"You are too young to know what you want.

That's why I think it best that you marry an older man. A mature person will look after you. Believe me, my dear, I am doing what is best for you," added Jeb kindly.

"You are not doing what is best for me! You are being selfish. The only reason you and Aunt wish me to marry him is so you and Caleb can make business deals. Why can't you just do it by yourselves? Or if someone has to marry him, let Aunt Elspeth do so, since she likes him so much. I'll stay home with you, Papa."

"That's a shocking way for a young girl to talk. Marry Elspeth indeed! You have merely proved that you are still a child. The sooner you and Caleb are married, the better. Your aunt and I seem to have failed with you, but perhaps Caleb will be able to curb your excesses."

Daphne was deeply hurt by her father's words. She wanted more than anything to please him, but she wouldn't do so at the price of her own happiness.

"I never will consent to marry him. Never!" she stormed.

"You may go to your room now, young lady. I see we'll have to treat you like a child."

"Oh, Papa, why must you try to force me in this? Why?"

"To your room, Daphne. You have to learn to accept authority. You will marry Caleb Winters and that is the end of the matter." Jeb's face had turned to stone and she knew there was no more appealing to him.

Daphne ran to her bedroom and threw herself on the bed, burying her head in the pillow. What had become of her loving father?

"Why do they treat me like a child? If I marry Caleb, I really think it will be the end of my life. I can't become like Catherine and that is just what he wants me to be. There must be a way out, there must be!" Daphne cried into her pillow.

Daphne then checked the watch that hung from her blouse. Only nine o'clock. Nearly three hours until it was time to leave to meet Tad at the old oak. Daphne sighed. She could barely wait to see her old friend and pour out her troubles to him.

She brooded until the chimes of the grandfather clock in the hallway struck eleven and interrupted her reverie. Daphne heard her father retire to his room and then heard Elspeth's quick, light step pause in front of Daphne's door. Elspeth listened, heard no sound, and then retreated. Daphne kept absolutely still until she heard her aunt enter her own room and shut the door. Then Daphne went to the window and peered out at the Allegheny River beyond the back garden. A full moon lit the river and its banks.

Even at this late hour, the city was still awake and the river was busy. A steamboat whistled far up the river. Daphne heard the train going up Liberty Street on its way to East Liberty and Oakland, the motorman ringing his bell. The sounds comforted her. Nothing could be too terrible as long as the city went about its business.

Time always passed quickly for Daphne when she daydreamed by the window. She imagined herself a boatman on the river, keeping watch over the barge; then a sleepy German mechanic, belly full of beer, walking home from the beer garden. Life looked so wonderful, so varied and exciting from the windows of her father's house on Lower Penn Street. It was wonderful to see so much life from a window.

It was eleven-thirty when Daphne put on her cloak and slipped quietly from the house in her stocking feet. At the back door she slipped on her boots and, keeping to the shadows, walked away from the house. She made her way along the river, through the back gardens of the other mansions on Lower Penn Street and then out onto Liberty Street. The old quarry was nearly a mile from her father's house and Daphne walked quickly to be on time. In a few minutes she was standing beside the old oak near the quarry. She looked around for Tad, but there was no sign of him.

Daphne was about to whistle their familiar signal when suddenly she heard voices coming down the path from the direction of Minersville. She hid in the hollow of the oak tree and waited for them to pass, reassuring herself that Tad would soon be there. But instead of going on past her, the men had stopped at the quarry and stood there talking.

The night was so still that she could have heard their every word, even if she had not been holding her breath.

"Are we all here?"

"No, Seamus ain't here yet."

"Gus neither."

"We can't wait."

"Yeah, let's start without 'em. Ain't no point in waiting for those two, when the lot of us might get caught if we stay too long."

"It's perfectly lawful for us to meet."

"Tain't lawful to unionize and you know it, Rene LeBrun."

"It should be, Amby. Why the constitution says . . ."

"Rene, Rene, none of yer speechifying. We got business to do."

"Aye."

"The meeting of the Minersville chapter of the Knights of Labor is hereby called to order."

The Knights of Labor! thought Daphne. Why, they're those men Papa is always saying are trying to form unions and take his money. They're like those Molly Maguire men, and very dangerous. She strained to hear better.

"I say we call a strike against the mine owners."

"Hear, hear," came the answering cry, yet Daphne detected sounds of dissent.

"Those who don't agree should speak up now," said the man who had called for the strike.

"I don't. What'll it gain us, Rene? I ask you, brothers, think of what happened in the Long Strike. The mine owners refused to negotiate and we had all those long months of hunger for nothing. We can't afford to strike. We'll lose and then we'll be worse off than we are now!"

"We're losing right at this very moment, Bob," answered the first man. "Every day that we work for less than we should, we're losing. The owners are robbing us and we're not even men enough to stop them. I call that pathetic.

"The strike is the only weapon of the workingman. The bosses won't appreciate how much our work is worth to them unless they don't have it for a while. They won't pay us what we're worth until they're forced to.

"Aren't you sick of living in broken-down, stinking company houses? Aren't you tired of never having enough money? Seeing your wife and children go without? Going down in mines that aren't safe and wondering if you'll come up again after your shift? We have no choice. We must fight for safe conditions and decent pay."

There were cries of agreement. Daphne longed to see what the great orator looked like. She leaned out of the hollow. As she did so, a twig snapped beneath her foot. She held her breath, hoping they hadn't heard.

"What was that?" a voice cried fearfully.

"Someone's spying on us," cried another man.

"Let's get him!" hollered a third.

Daphne shrank farther back into the tree trunk, praying that they wouldn't find her in the darkness. Suddenly a lantern appeared before her and a man growled, "Out with you, young man."

"Don't touch me," said Daphne with as much dignity as she could muster.

"Doggone! If it ain't a girl."

The man took Daphne's arm and led her back to the others, who all seemed dumbfounded by her presence.

"What be you doing here, young miss?" asked a bearded giant of a man in a puzzled tone.

Daphne looked around her, too startled and frightened to say anything. If they were like the Molly Maguires, they might kill her. Yet they didn't look like murderers at all: just ordinary workingmen.

"Doubtless she is waiting for a beau, who has

doubtless stood her up. Isn't that so," said a darkly handsome young man coming forward from the shadows beneath a tree. Daphne recognized his voice as that of the man who had given the rousing speech in favor of striking.

"I most certainly was not," replied Daphne, piqued that he should have guessed right so easily and suddenly aware of the impropriety of meeting a man in the woods at that hour.

"Then perhaps you would like to admit being a spy for the mine owners?"

"I am not a spy."

"Then how do you explain your presence here, if I may be so bold as to enquire."

"You may not," snapped Daphne. "One does not cross-examine a lady."

"True, but ladies do not frequent tree trunks at midnight."

"No need to frighten the lass, Rene."

"Sure there is," responded a rough-looking man. "And what would she be doing here in the middle of the night if she weren't a spy or a hussy?"

The others laughed and Daphne's cheeks burned.

"I think I shall be going home now," she said as calmly as she could.

"Not so fast, missy," warned another man, gripping her arm.

"You're hurting me."

"What are you doing here?" The man shook her.

"Leave her be, Stan," said the bearded orator, Rene, in a tone of authority. "As I said, the lady obviously had a romantic assignation. One which, I may add, has disappointed her. Her young man has failed to appear at the appointed hour. Isn't that so? I think you had better swallow your pride and admit it before my friends here treat you as a spy."

Daphne's cheeks burned and she nodded.

Satisfied, Rene sighed, "I think we'd best clear out in case the fellow she's waiting for turns up. I'll accompany the lady to her home."

The men began to move off and soon they were gone.

"Where do you live?"

"Lower Penn Street," mumbled Daphne.

"Take my arm and pull your cloak around your face so that no one can see you," her escort ordered as they set off.

From beneath her hood, Daphne scrutinized the man. He had long, dark brown hair and a thick, dark brown beard. His lips were full and curved in a perpetual sardonic grin. Heavy brows grew nearly together and cast his grey eyes in shadow. His cheekbones were high and his nose aquiline. He looked artistic, even dashing, but his hands were those of a workingman's, square-fingered and calloused, scarred by laboring in the mines.

After a few steps, Daphne decided that she would rather not be in the debt of this insolent young man for walking her home. At any rate, they were nearly out of the woods and at Liberty Street.

"I think I can proceed on my own, thank you," said Daphne politely, attempting to disengage her arm from his.

"I think not. It is too late for you to be out on your own. I can't think how your family permits it."

"They don't!" exclaimed Daphne, shocked by the idea of Aunt Elspeth allowing her out in the middle of the night. "Why, I sneak out."

The young man did not trouble to suppress his laughter.

"Liberty Street is perfectly safe and well lit," Daphne persisted.

"I cannot permit you to go alone," the young man responded firmly.

The two continued on in silence. Daphne felt awkward. It seemed there was nothing to do but allow him to walk her home. She decided to try to learn more about this Rene.

"You seem to know all about me, but I know nothing about you," Daphne began. "I'm not as good at guessing as you are, so you must tell me."

"I must, must I? What do you need to know?" questioned Rene, a glimmer of amusement in his eyes.

"Why, your name to start. Your friends call you Rene."

"I can't tell you my name. Suppose you really are a spy. You might tell the police that you saw me."

"Why should I want to do that?"

"Perhaps you don't believe that workingmen should form unions."

"But why should that be a matter for the police?"

"It was in '73. The Molly Maguires," he added, not missing the frown on Daphne's face.

"The Molly Maguires weren't just getting together to talk about a union. They were planning to kill people."

"Perhaps. Perhaps not. They were killed for their plans. Hanged by the neck until dead."

Daphne and Rene walked on in silence, there being no way to talk comfortably of men who had been hanged just down the road at the corner of

Market Street. After a while he asked, "And what about your name?"

"It's Daphne." She saw no reason not to answer.

"What were you doing out by the old quarry?"

"I was waiting for a friend, but he didn't arrive."

"So you do have a sweetheart."

"Oh, no," giggled Daphne, imagining Tad as a sweetheart, "just an old friend, home from the university, who wanted to talk to me."

"Do you always meet people by tree stumps at night? In another time, you would have been burned as a witch for doing that."

"We used to meet there when we were children. I wanted so much to talk to him," she explained wistfully.

"Is something troubling you?"

"My father wants me to marry a man I hate. I can't marry Caleb Winters and I won't."

"Caleb Winters?" asked Rene in a hollow voice.

"Do you know him?"

"I work in his mine, the thieving dog. He worked a friend of mine almost to death. He employs children to do work that's too hard for most men. He is responsible for more misery than any other man I can think of."

"I admit I never liked him, but I never thought he was quite that awful. I only wonder why my father wishes me to marry him."

"Who is your father?"

"Jebediah Slater," answered Daphne proudly.

There was a long silence before Rene responded.

"He is as evil as Caleb Winters, and he also profits from misery. Your father is a scoundrel and a thief."

"How dare you say such a thing!" cried Daphne. "He is the most honest man I know, not a thug like you and your friends. He works harder than anyone."

Rene laughed bitterly.

"You may unhand me now, sir," Daphne said coldly. "This is my home."

"As you wish, my lady," he responded in a voice laden with sarcasm. "So this is the famous Slater mansion! Good night to you. And mind you don't go out in the woods at night."

Daphne was too furious to reply and turned away abruptly. She sneaked around the house and found the kitchen entry. There was no time to consider her escort, for a familiar bony hand grabbed her arm and she heard the familiar voice. "Where have you been, you sneaking chit?"

Chapter 3

"Aunt Elspeth!" cried Daphne. "What are you doing awake?"

"One might ask the same of you. Where have you been?"

Daphne kept silent in an effort to collect her wits. Her aunt would hardly believe any story she made up and Daphne was hesitant to tell her the truth for fear she would be severely scolded. The best course, she reasoned, was to keep silent.

"Don't stand there staring at me like a stick, girl. I demand that you tell me where you have been. Out with it."

"I can't tell you, Aunt."

"You mean you won't. You have always been willful and stubborn. I have told your father over and over that your nature must be curbed. This is the result! Out in the middle of the night like the most brazen hussy! You tell me where you have been and with whom," hissed Elspeth, her fingers gripping Daphne's arm.

"I couldn't sleep, so I went out into the back garden to look at the river."

"Don't think that you can deceive me with that feeble tale. You were not alone. Who was that man?"

Daphne started. Her aunt had seen him!

"So this is why you refuse to marry Caleb! You have a lover—some lowborn person, I have no doubt. You must give him up and do your duty to the family that has loved and cherished you from birth."

"I can't, Aunt," Daphne insisted. "I can't."

"That is because you are an unnatural brat and always have been. You inherit it from your mother, I suppose. I warned Jeb not to marry her, but he refused to listen to me and now look at the result! A brazen hussy of a daughter gadding about in the middle of the night with one knows not whom. If I were not a woman of strong constitution and determined mentality, I might tremble at the sight of such things. You will promise me that you will give up this man and marry Caleb or I will tell your father all!"

"There was no man there, I can assure you, Aunt, but as to marrying Caleb Winters, that I can never do."

"Then I shall have to tell your father what I have seen."

"And what have you seen, Aunt? You have seen me out for a walk in the back garden and you have seen a shadow that your eye perceived as a man. I was alone, I tell you!"

"I don't believe you, but your father will. He always takes your part. You remind him of her," sighed Aunt Elspeth in tones of distaste. "You must promise

me never to see that man again. I'll be watching to
see that you keep your promise. You have not tricked
me now anymore than you ever could. You were a
wicked child and you have grown to be a wicked
woman, despite all I could do for you."

"You have done nothing for me," cried Daphne,
losing her patience. "You have never liked me, not
since I was a child. Why must you always criticize,
Aunt? Our natures are not alike, and it seems we can
never be pleased with one another."

"We can. You could marry Caleb."

"Marry Caleb! Marry Caleb! Can we never speak
of anything else? I am sick to death of Caleb. I wish I
had never heard of him. Can't you and my father see
how wrong it would be for me to marry a man I feel
so strongly against?"

"You feel strongly against him because you are a
rebellious and contrary child and always have been.
Caleb is just the sort of man you require. You will
soon be as sweet and docile as his sister Catherine."

Her aunt's cold gaze bored into Daphne's back as
she left the kitchen. Daphne knew that she would be
watched in the days ahead. Why had she not understood that she and Tad were too old now to meet at
the quarry?

The next morning, after a tense breakfast with
her aunt and father, Daphne went into the conservatory, happy to tend the plants. Removing dead leaves
and flowers, making sure they had not overgrown
their pots, always absorbed her attention. Before long,
Daphne heard a knock at the door and Tad was
shown into the conservatory by Hawkins.

"Tad!" greeted Daphne, holding out her hands to him. "How wonderful to see you. You're so grown up!"

Tad twirled his straw boater in his hands self-consciously and shifted from one long leg to the other, peering nervously at Daphne from behind his thick, steel-rimmed glasses. Suddenly a broad grin lit his thin, serious face and he blurted out, "You haven't changed at all! Still the same imp, your hands and face all dirty, just as when we were children. Come, let me wipe your face."

"Am I dirty? I was repotting a plant and could hardly help getting a bit of dirt on my hands."

"Naturally not!" replied Tad, wiping her face with his pocket handkerchief. He looked fondly into her eyes. Daphne returned his gaze frankly and openly.

"Enough of this foolishness," she said, drawing away. "Tell me why you didn't meet me last night after I went to all the trouble of going to the oak. It was cruel of you to leave me in a hollow tree in the dead of night."

"I am sorry, Daphne, but it couldn't be helped. Mother insisted on talking to me until half past one in the morning. She has decided I must learn all about the business now that I am grown. And you know Mother . . . no putting her off till tomorrow what one can do today. My head was positively spinning with all the figures she would try to fill it with. Mother is a remarkable woman; I think no man could manage the business as well as she does."

"But now you must tell me what it is you were so anxious to speak to me about."

"All in good time, my child."

38

"Don't talk to me in that condescending manner, Tad. I am nearly as old as you are, you know."

"No. I am nearly three years older. And I have been to Harvard."

"Where you became insufferable."

"Same old Daphne. Shall I tell you about life at the great college?"

"Yes, do," said Daphne, leading him to a pair of wicker chairs near the fountain and under a large palm. It was far from the door, so if Aunt Elspeth passed by, she would not hear them.

"Boston is the most wonderful city," Tad began eagerly. "Even nicer than Pittsburgh. There is ever so much to do. So many concerts and lectures and learned men. We hear all the best speakers there and see the most famous theatrical people. Sarah Bernhardt has played there."

"She's played here, too, you snob. I saw her."

"And Harvard is wonderful, too, Daphne. I've studied under William James, the famous philosopher, and have learned such a lot. And such amazing libraries. We have nothing in Pittsburgh to compare. All the men here are concerned only with business and leave culture entirely to the ladies. Whereas in Boston, everyone is concerned with the arts and drama and letters. In many ways, I'm sorry to be back home."

"How can you say that? Pittsburgh is so exciting! There is so much activity. People make their fortunes here every day inventing new, wondrous things. You had only to go to the Centennial Exposition in Philadelphia last year to see that nearly half of what was there had been made in Pittsburgh. I think I could never trade the excitement and noise and bustle of Pittsburgh for any other city. And it is so healthful here. Since coal dust protects the lungs, we have no malaria or contagious diseases."

"Daphne, you have hardly traveled, and you are too young to be so firmly decided in favor of one place. You must keep an open mind."

"People always are telling me I am too young," sighed Daphne. "Papa and Aunt Elspeth treat me as a child and try to make all decisions for me. Don't you think it's wrong of them, Tad?"

"What decisions are they trying to make?"

She took a deep breath, then told him the problem. "I had supposed you would have heard. They want me to marry Caleb Winters. They think it's my duty, but I don't believe that something so much against my nature can be my duty. Isn't my duty to myself higher than that to my parents?"

"You are going to marry Caleb?" asked Tad in disbelief.

"I see you, at least, are on my side."

"I don't think you and Caleb will suit in the least. This goes against all my plans, all I have dreamed of. I love you and always will. I couldn't bear to see you married to another."

Daphne was stunned. Was he serious?

"I've thought of nothing but you for the past year," he continued. "That's why I wanted to meet with you last night. I wanted to ask you to be mine."

"But . . ." Daphne cast around for the right words. "We've always been such good friends, Tad. I can't possibly envision any other relationship between us."

"That's just it, Daphne. We've always gotten along so well. Since I've been out in the world a bit, I realize that you are the only woman I could ever care for. Daphne, please say you will be mine."

"I can't, Tad."

"But why? Is it because you consider yourself betrothed to Caleb?"

"No. I won't marry him. I don't love you, Tad," Daphne said softly. "I care for you a great deal, but only as a brother and a friend."

"That is worse than nothing at all!" exclaimed Tad. "It's cruel to deny someone who loves you as I do the privilege of loving and caring for you."

"It would be cruel to marry you without loving you," responded Daphne gently, but firmly.

"Please, Daphne, consider carefully whether you can possibly come to love me. I believe I could never be happy without you."

"Don't say such an awful thing. We will be friends once again."

"But if you married me, you wouldn't have to marry Caleb. Surely your father would approve of a match between us."

"No, he is so set on my marrying Caleb. And besides, I could never do such a thing to you."

"In that case," Tad declared stoutly, "I will love you from afar. I'll write you love poems every day."

The dejected Tad soon took his leave and Daphne ordered tea to be brought to the drawing room. When the hot toast and tea arrived, she ate with great pleasure. Considering two suitors in as many days had given her a hearty appetite.

While she sipped her tea, she heard the sounds of arguing in the kitchen yard and she went to investigate. Cook and Hawkins were in the yard with a thin, shabbily dressed, dark-haired young girl who looked about fifteen years old. The girl's eyes flashed and her face was flushed.

"No," said the girl firmly in accented English. "I want work. Please. Strong girl. Work good."

"I'll attend to this, Hawkins," Daphne called. "Cook, bring a tray of tea into the small drawing room." Before either Cook or Hawkins could protest, Daphne beckoned to the girl and she followed Daphne into the house and to the small drawing room.

As they entered the room, the girl stared around in amazement. Her eyes roamed about the elegantly furnished room, the brightly colored Oriental rugs and the ornately carved furniture. At last she looked back at Daphne, whom she admired just as openly.

The girl was small, a little over five feet tall, with wiry arms that hung far beyond the sleeves of her thin grey cotton dress. Straight blonde hair hung loosely over her shoulder. Sharp brown eyes were set deeply beneath heavy brows. Her nose was flat, her worst feature by far. Her cheekbones were high and broad, while her mouth was full and gentle.

"Now then," said Daphne when the tea had been served and she saw the girl had taken her first ravenous bites. "What is your name?"

"Hedwig Bronislavski."

"Where are you from?"

"Poland," replied the girl proudly, "but now I am an American."

"Then you need an American name. Do you mind if I call you Heddie?"

"Heddie is nice," the girl smiled. "Very American."

"Now, Heddie, you want to work here? What can you do?"

"Anything, I work hard, very strong girl. Can do all work."

"I hate to see someone who wants to work go without employment. You can work here. I'll arrange it with my aunt when she comes home later."

"Thank you, miss, thank you. I need work so much."

"Here, have another cake," offered Daphne warmly.

"I am not hungry for more. I take it home if you don't need."

"By all means."

"Mama and Stan and Casimir and Mary Ann and Cecilia and Jan and Maria and Stefan can all taste."

"They won't get very much of such a small cake."

"My family is hungry and now I have work. We can eat better, miss."

"No wonder you look thin! I'll send you home with a basket of food."

"Oh, thank you, miss."

"Soon you'll be working for your living, Heddie, and won't be so thin anymore." Daphne desperately wanted to help Heddie's family, but charity wasn't what they really needed.

"Who are all those people you were talking about before?"

"My little brothers and sisters. Stan and Stefan work already in the coal mines, but the rest is too little for this. I try factory work but am not so strong as they and fall down. But I am strong now, can do lots work, miss."

"Where do you live?"

"In Bayardstown," answered Heddie, naming the worst neighborhood in Pittsburgh. "We got nice room."

"All of you in one room?" inquired Daphne, shocked at the idea.

"A little crowded but not so bad. Is lovely here. I like to work here."

"I'm sure you'll do very well, Heddie. I'll like having you here. I'll go tell Cook to make you up a basket for all your brothers and sisters and then you can go home. Tomorrow I'll come visit you and tell you when you can start."

Chapter 4

Daphne was certain that her father would allow Heddie to be employed in some way. Whether Aunt Elspeth would agree was another matter. She was particular about servants, insisting that even the lowest scullery maid have proper references. Still, if her father said yes, Daphne did not see how her aunt could refuse.

That matter being entirely settled in her mind, Daphne considered how she and Heddie would get on. She had never met a girl like Heddie and was extremely curious to know all about her life. It was bound to be so different from her own. Just think of the excitement of traveling all the way from Poland to begin a new life in America! Daphne tried to picture the voyage across the Atlantic in the huge steamer, the bewildering crush of people in New York, the trip to Pittsburgh, the crowded room Heddie and her family now lived in.

Daphne was startled from her musings when her

father and aunt entered the drawing room. Since they had begun to press Caleb's suit upon her, Daphne had come to dread the evenings they were together. Tremendous arguments always ensued. Daphne had an independent spirit, but not a quarrelsome one, and she disliked having to be at odds with her father. There seemed to be no avoiding it, however. Better to be at odds with her father for a few months than at odds with Caleb Winters for the rest of her life!

"Good evening, Daphne. Have you had a pleasant day?" her father asked.

"Oh, yes, Papa. I met the most delightful girl. She came to the back door of the house looking for work and said she would not leave until she had found it. Isn't that spirited of her? And I went out and spoke to her and she told me how she had just come to America and had to support her brothers and sisters. I think we should give her some work. Can we, please, Papa? She is the dearest girl and ever so strong and willing to work."

"Well," laughed her father. "I suppose we must have something she could do."

Aunt Elspeth proved more difficult to convince, but Daphne and her father had their way. At the end of the evening Daphne was pleased to find that dinner had passed pleasantly, with no mention of Caleb at all. They sat by the fire, Aunt Elspeth sewing, and Daphne and her father playing cribbage. It reminded Daphne of the happy old days before Caleb's plans to marry her had ruined everything.

The next morning Daphne awoke to the sounds of sweeping and scrubbing and feet running up and down steps. Elspeth Slater's voice rose and fell, issuing orders to various servants. Daphne leapt out of bed, anxious to go into town to meet Catherine Winters and pick up her new ball gown. Tonight all of Pittsburgh would be in the Slater mansion for the elaborate dinner her father was giving.

A little later, as Daphne sorted impatiently through her mail, which contained the usual invitations and courtesy notes, she came upon an envelope addressed to "Miss Dafna."

Odd, thought Daphne as she ripped the letter open. Who could this be from? And then she read the following:

Be careful, mum, or else! Do not cross us. We mean it. Sined, K of L.

"Why, it's from those men I met in the woods the other night. How dare they threaten me! Nonsense!" Yet she couldn't suppress a shudder as she watched the page catch fire and burn in the grate, the letters growing larger and more sinister the moment before they burned. Daphne drew a deep breath and collected her thoughts.

Her spirits returned an hour later when she arrived at the dressmaker's shop. She was always delighted to see Madame Rouen, the Frenchwoman, for she was such a neat, tidy little person. Always in black dresses, her hair pulled back in a snood, she reminded Daphne of a schoolmarm. Her dark eyes darted about the room and she chattered brightly.

Catherine had arrived some time before Daphne. She was wearing her gown and having the final tucks fitted by Madame herself. Catherine looked so wraith-like in the light blue satin gown with its duchess lace overlays. It accentuated her frailty, making her seem a fairy tale princess instead of a sickly young woman. This was all Madame Rouen's doing, as Daphne well knew. Before Daphne had introduced Catherine to Madame, her gowns had always been dismal.

"Why, Catherine, you look lovely! Like some beautiful creature from the spirit world," cried Daphne, taking Catherine's arms and holding them out to study the blue gown.

"Do you think so?" her friend asked nervously. "I find the neckline much too daring and not at all flattering with my thin chest, but Madame Rouen has suggested that a bit of netting will soften it."

"*Ma chérie*, you are a vision. Mademoiselle Daphne will be very sorry when all the young men flock to you. I have made you into a belle, yes?"

"Oh, I hardly think so, Madame. Daphne is the belle of Pittsburgh."

"Not tonight, Catherine. The gown suits you too well," Daphne smiled. "May I see my gown, Madame?"

"Of course, *ma chérie*. Marie, help mademoiselle into her gown."

Daphne left for the dressing room. When she saw herself in the mirror, she realized that Madame Rouen had created a gown even more beautiful than the one she had imagined.

The long train of pink taffeta brocaded in silver thread trailed behind her, the rose pattern glinting as she moved. The bodice was made of the same pink taffeta and cut very low. Puffs of pink satin over the hips were drawn back to form the bustle. The underskirt was also of satin, trimmed with a deep border of pearl beadwork and a bead-and-silk fringe. Daphne was tall enough to wear the dress well. She leaned forward toward the mirror and plucked at the puffed sleeves, setting their silver fringes bobbing, then turned and admired her swelling bosom.

"Truly, if I wear dresses like this all the time, I'll become very vain. Madame Rouen, you are a magician."

"Mademoiselle is pleased?" the dressmaker inquired.

"Oh, very! I have never seen such a lovely dress!"

Daphne remained absolutely still as Madame Rouen's fingers flew over the gown, straightening and pinning until it fit Daphne as well as her own skin. When there was no more to be done, she and Catherine left Madame Rouen, their cries of gratitude ringing in the store.

Daphne and Catherine walked arm in arm toward Market Street. It was a beautiful summer day, the blue sky showing between clouds of soot that nearly hid the sun. Pittsburgh's factories were operating at full speed, her chimneys spewing coal dust into the city. Daphne and Catherine were so accustomed to it that they barely noticed the constant need to brush soot and ash off their summer frocks and bonnets.

"I'm sure it will be quite a brilliant party, and the dancing will be such fun for you, my dear Daphne."

"And also for you, Catherine."

"Oh, no, dancing is too spirited for me. I don't have the constitution to bear too much excitement. Oh, if I had your health and temperament, Daphne, how exciting life would be!"

"Don't talk nonsense, Catherine. You've been in quite good health since recovering from that attack of pleurisy."

"Oh, Daphne, I know I shouldn't complain, but I seem to suffer so from migraines. Caleb thinks them all imaginary, but the pain is so real."

"You don't have a migraine now, do you, Catherine? I have some salts in my reticule."

"No, I feel quite well. Your high spirits always seem to overflow onto me and cheer me as well. I wish you and I were sisters. You are the dearest creature I know, Daphne."

"We really are rather like sisters, aren't we?" Daphne laughed as she squeezed her friend's hand.

"Yes, but we aren't very much alike. Why, even as we walk down this street I'm afraid, but you aren't bothered at all."

"Why, what do you mean?"

"All these idle men standing around the streets. We are receiving considerable attention."

"They mean no harm," said Daphne. "Papa says these are hard times and that those men are out of work. They stand about on the corners hoping to hear of jobs."

"I have heard rumors that they may cause trouble. They're so poor and hungry. You've heard all the talk of strikes and all the agitation for societies of workingmen."

"Yes, but I take no notice of it. Workingmen want to cooperate with their employers to create better conditions for them both. Despite these hard times we are passing through, I think there's no need to fear them."

"But what of such groups as the Molly Maguires and their treacherous actions against their employers in the mines?"

"They were severely punished to deter others

from a similar attempt, were they not? Hanging from the neck until dead—that's pretty severe punishment."

Catherine spoke up abruptly. "Is it my imagination, or is that man over there staring at you? Do you know him?"

"No," responded Daphne too quickly, trying to keep her voice level, forcing herself to gaze directly into her friend's eyes, "I have never seen the man."

"Odd, how he looks at you," Catherine persisted.

"It is mere presumption on his part," said Daphne, hurrying Catherine along into a shop, where she changed the subject and tried to forget the shock of seeing the man who had walked her home from the woods. He had looked at her so piercingly. As though he were watching her. Perhaps he had sent the letter.

No, I can't believe that. He's not a coward who would send anonymous threats through the mail, thought Daphne to herself, barely aware of Catherine's chattering.

After bidding her friend farewell until the evening, Daphne took the East Liberty Passenger Railway as far as the Sixteenth Street Bridge and then set out, carrying a large parcel, through the streets of Bayardstown in search of Heddie's home. Although Daphne had lived in Pittsburgh all her life, she had never before ventured into Bayardstown. It was a poor neighborhood, rife with crime, disease and drink. The streets were narrow and dirty. Sewage flowed down the middle of the unpaved streets toward the Allegheny River where the boys, the Bayardstown Rats as they were called, bathed naked. The whole neighborhood reeked of sickness and death. Epidemics were frequent and each winter many died of scarlet fever and pneumonia in the damp, crowded, unsanitary rooms.

Daphne, living only a mile to the south of this squalor, had known almost nothing of it. As she walked the narrow, filthy streets between rows of dilapidated wooden tenements that towered shakily above her, it almost seemed as though she had entered another world.

Daphne finally located Heddie's tenement, a nearly windowless wooden building set in a dirty yard. A group of children splashed in the mud around the water faucet that served the whole tenement. They directed Daphne to a back room on the fourth floor. Daphne climbed the rickety stairs of the jerry-built house, feeling ill from the poorly ventilated rooms. How could such a place be considered fit to live in?

Daphne knocked and immediately Heddie's cheerful face appeared, wreathed in smiles.

"I told them you was coming. But nobody believe it. Can I work for you?"

"Of course," replied Daphne, stepping into the small room. "In fact, you may come with me now and start immediately."

"Oh, Mama," cried Heddie joyously, running to a thin, exhausted-looking woman lying in a narrow bed. Daphne followed slowly.

Heddie spoke quickly to her mother and then turned to Daphne. "I am sorry to speak Polish when you don't know it, but Mama hasn't got any English. She is very happy now I got work and she say you are a very pretty lady and good to have me."

"Please tell your mother that we're delighted you

are coming to work for us. I only hope you'll be happy."

"When I work and we eat, then I am happy, but I tell Mama," said Heddie, turning once again to speak to her mother.

Mrs. Bronislavski lifted herself weakly from the pillows and held out her thin hands to Daphne. Taking both of Daphne's hands in her frail, cool ones, she whispered, "Tank you," and fell back against her pillow.

"Poor Mama, she so tired all the time. But soon she have the new baby Papa left us and she be well, yes, Mama?" said Heddie, tears filling her eyes. She suspected that the exhausted Mrs. Bronislavski would never be well again. It was then that Daphne realized that Mrs. Bronislavski was with child and nearing the end of her confinement.

"I brought you some more food until you have earned enough money to buy your own. And here is a dress for you, Heddie."

Heddie accepted the old cotton print dress as though it were the finest Paris fashion. She held it up against her grey, shapeless dress and looked down to admire it. Then Heddie ran from the room, clutching the dress.

Daphne sat stiffly in a chair by the door, smiling hesitantly at Heddie's mother. She was, for once, at a loss for words and curious as to why Heddie had left the room so suddenly. She soon became aware of several pairs of watchful brown eyes that belonged to Daphne's brothers and sisters. She smiled at them and leaned over to chuck the smallest child under the chin, but he retreated in fright to his mother's side.

Daphne then occupied herself by looking around

the room. The little home was as clean as regular scrubbing could make it, but no amount of care could brighten the dark, airless place. It was no wonder that Heddie's mother had become ill.

Daphne's meditations were interrupted by the reappearance of Heddie, clad in her new finery. She twirled about the room, laughing and preening herself before her mother, chattering in Polish.

"You look lovely, Heddie," Daphne ventured, hating to interrupt, "but I think it's time for us to go. I'm expected home and Aunt will want to instruct you in your duties."

"Yes, miss, I'm ready," replied Heddie, and with that the two departed the dingy tenement.

Heddie chattered to Daphne the whole way back in the streetcar and after a while Daphne said, "I think we'll get along very well, Heddie, but you must understand that my Aunt Elspeth manages the house and she can be very stern. You must listen very closely to everything she says and do exactly as she tells you. And you and I will have lessons every day so you can improve your English."

"Oh, you are so good to me! Someday, I live too in a big house with Mama and all the rest, and I give work to poor girls. This is America!"

"Perhaps, Heddie, who can say?"

Chapter 5

After placing Heddie in Cook's care, Daphne flew up the polished stairs to her room to be sure that her ball gown had arrived safely.

Letty was just laying it out on the bed, her careful fingers straightening out tiny wrinkles.

"Miss Daphne!" exclaimed Letty. "I never saw such a beautiful dress. Why, the men will flock about you like bees to honey."

"Madame Rouen has done marvelously with it and it does look good on me, even if I say so myself."

"But your shoes are all muddy. Where have you been?"

"To Bayardstown."

"Bayardstown! Why, whatever for? That's no place for a young lady. Your aunt will be so angry."

"I only went to find Heddie and tell her that she could come to work for us. They live in the most dreadful house, Letty. You would not think that people would live so in this day and age. I was quite shocked.

59

I think my aunt wastes her time knitting for people in Africa when there are people right here in Pittsburgh in such terrible need. Still, Heddie is well established now, and she should soon be able to help her family move to a better place."

"If she can manage to keep her position here," muttered Letty darkly.

"Why should she not? She is most willing and I do not doubt but that she will prove able as well."

"As you wish, Miss Daphne," said Letty leaning over the ball gown once more and straightening imaginary creases.

"Don't be tiresome, Letty. I can always tell when you do busy work in that fatiguing way that you have something more to say. Please come out with it!"

"Well, since you asked me most particularly, I may say. You won't think I'm being a gossip?"

"No, Letty. Tell me."

"Well, I've heard that your Polish girl isn't welcome in this house. Not by any means. Cook resents the way you stepped in and so does Hawkins. They're that proud, those two. And your aunt don't like it none, neither. The rest of us below stairs don't think much of Poles. We think they's dirty."

"That's enough!" said Daphne sharply. "There's nothing different about the Polish. We are all God's children."

"Yes, miss, but all God's children ain't the same," replied Letty stubbornly.

"You do vex me at times, Letty. Now, I want you to tell me anything you hear about Heddie. Try to help her, and please be kind to her."

At that instant Elspeth Slater entered the room in

what Daphne always referred to as "one of her fire-breathing states."

"I thought I'd find you two up here gabbing away while I am running around the house doing the work of ten men preparing for this party and simultaneously training the most slovenly creature God ever put on this earth. I suppose I may look to the next world for my reward because I'll certainly find no peace in this one," finished Elspeth in trumpeting tones.

"I am sorry, Aunt. I was just seeing to my gown."

"That bit of frippery," sniffed Elspeth. "Well, if you can spare a bit of time from vanity and gossip, I would appreciate your seeing to the flower arrangements in the drawing room."

"Yes, Aunt." Daphne hurried after Elspeth and ran down the steps.

"And do not run about like a hoyden. Decorum, decorum," scolded Elspeth.

Elspeth vanished into the dining room and the chatter of the housemaids working in there stopped instantly. Daphne went into the drawing room, picked up the two Chinese vases that sat on either side of the mantelpiece, and carefully carried them into the conservatory. Soon she was happily at work arranging scarlet roses, yellow dahlias, orange gladioli and tiger lilies, and greens. It would be a glorious display.

Her solitude was interrupted all too soon when Letty rushed into the conservatory and cried, "Miss Daphne, if there ain't a ruckus in the kitchen and it's all that Heddie's fault. She's broke your aunt's best crystal glasses what was going out on the table. I told you as she'd come to no good in this house."

Daphne ran from the room to see if she could mediate between Heddie and her aunt, and her heart sank when she reached the kitchen. Heddie knelt on the floor, sobbing amid thousands of glistening crystal shards. She was trying to sweep them up while Elspeth Slater, Cook and Hawkins stood over her, their voices competing. The rest of the serving maids stood around the kitchen, goggle-eyed in astonishment at the scene before them.

Daphne rushed into the fray. "Aunt Elspeth, please, calm yourself. It doesn't do for you to become overexcited."

"You, Daphne, brought this clumsy oaf of a girl into the house. Now look what she's done. My best crystal, imported from England, all smashed."

"Not all, surely, Aunt. Why, there is another tray of glasses there and more on the table. It was a mishap that Heddie dropped the tray, but accidents do occur and she surely didn't mean to break them."

Cook and Hawkins had been silenced by Daphne's entrance. Elspeth realized that all the servants were staring at the two of them. She struggled to calm herself.

"Very well, we will not discuss it further. Heddie, you will leave this house instantly. I cannot have such a clumsy girl serving here."

Heddie's imploring, tear-stained face and huge, dark eyes turned toward Daphne in silent appeal. Daphne sympathized with her, yet there seemed no way of placating her aunt.

"Aunt, please give Heddie another chance. Please," pleaded Daphne, doubtful that her entreaties would carry much weight.

"Very well. You, Heddie, sweep up that glass and

stop crying. I trust that in the future you'll take greater care. Tomorrow I shall attempt to find you more suitable work. For tonight, you may assist Cook by washing the pots."

"Thank you, ma'am," said Heddie to Elspeth, darting a grateful glance in Daphne's direction.

Sighing, Daphne went upstairs to dress for the party.

After Daphne had bathed and dressed, Letty set to work on Daphne's long strawberry-blonde hair, brushing it out vigorously and then pinning it up one section at a time. She formed a complicated pattern of waterfalls and spirals at the back of Daphne's head. The front was brushed back smoothly from Daphne's face. Across the crown of her head, at the very highest part of the bun, Letty pinned a row of fresh pink rosebuds. She stepped back to admire her handiwork, pulled a wrinkle from Daphne's dress, and finally was satisfied. "See that you don't break too many hearts, miss. And mind that neckline, it's a bit daring. I suppose you won't put a bit of lace fichu there to cover yourself a bit."

"Oh, no, Letty! It would ruin the dress. It's the latest fashion. Everyone wears low necks these days."

"Well, enjoy yourself, my dear."

Daphne rushed down the stairs, her high-heeled silver slippers catching the light from the chandeliers. She walked more sedately as she approached her father and Aunt Elspeth, who were standing by the door of the drawing room ready to receive their guests.

"My dear, you are a vision," said her father, kissing her cheek.

"A bit forward-looking," sniffed her aunt, staring

pointedly at the gown's low neckline and quickly bringing her hand up to be sure that her own neckline was fastened securely at the chin. Elspeth Slater was the picture of propriety in her stiff, garnet-colored dress of water-marked silk with its moderate bustle and high collar.

"I think it quite suits Daphne. She'll be the belle of the ball," observed Jeb. "You look like a fashion plate."

Daphne glowed at her father's praise and had a brief, childish urge to thrust her tongue out at her aunt.

For the next half-hour Daphne stood at the door, greeting each of her guests. Just as she was beginning to be bored, her father smilingly dismissed her. Daphne sought her friends and began to enjoy the party. Happily, Tad Billinghurst had recovered from their argument and greeted her warmly. Catherine Winters smiled shyly from across the room. Daphne walked into the crowded salon, conscious that tonight she was possessed of a special beauty. Before she had gone ten steps into the room, however, a piercing voice called out to her, freezing the smile on her lips.

"Why . . . Mrs. Humphreyville," Daphne stammered with as much grace as she could muster.

"Don't stand there gawking at me like a loon, girl. Do your duty as a hostess. Can't you see that I'm all alone and want talking to?" exclaimed cantankerous old Mrs. Humphreyville in such booming tones that the entire room turned around to stare. "What have you got to say for yourself, my girl?" demanded the old lady, pressing a large decorated tin horn to her good ear.

"You're looking well this evening, ma'am."

"Nonsense. Sick as a dog. I doubt I'll live through the summer."

"Oh, really! I can hardly think that . . . I mean you can't say such things."

"Why not? Everyone else does. My nephews are always prancing about, hanging on for their inheritance. Everyone thinks I'm dying," she finished with satisfaction.

In the long silence that followed, Daphne cast about for another subject of conversation. There was no pleasing Mrs. Humphreyville. After long years of experience, the old woman had come to realize the superiority of her own views over anyone else's. Consequently, she would disagree even if someone ventured to agree with her.

Daphne's discomfort was increased by her awareness of blue eyes watching her closely from across the room. Caleb loitered against the fireplace, one hand carelessly toying with his gold watch chain, the other arm resting against the marble mantelpiece. He was smirking insufferably at Daphne.

"Speak up, girl, I can't hear you!" shouted the irascible old lady.

"I didn't say anything," answered Daphne loudly.

"What?" cried Mrs. Humphreyville, thrusting the tin horn toward Daphne.

"I didn't say anything," shouted Daphne into it.

"No need to shout. Especially nonsense. You young girls these days are brought up without any conversation skills. Your case is worse, of course, being practically an orphan and with such a mother as you had. Your aunt has done her best by you, I will say that. Stuffed full of learning and I can't get a sentence out of you. I don't know what this world's coming to and I must say I'm glad to be leaving it."

"Will you go up to Point Breeze soon for the summer?" inquired Daphne politely.

"You must be more simple than I thought. Positively unhealthy to move up there before the Fourth of July. I never go up there before that, never have and never will," said Mrs. Humphreyville with considerable satisfaction at the thought of her own steady and well-regulated habits.

At that moment, the dinner gong rang and Mr. Humphreyville was summoned to escort his wife to dinner. Caleb and Tad both appeared at Daphne's elbow. An argument was averted when Tad's mother swept up, skirts crackling, and demanded that her son escort her to the table.

"I have you to myself at last," Caleb grinned, drawing Daphne's arm possessively through his. "You do look lovely."

"I'm not interested in foolish compliments, sir. If you are so gallant, why did you not rescue me from that old harridan?"

"I'm shocked to here you speak so of Pittsburgh's most respected lady! The reason I didn't rescue you was that it was much more amusing to watch you get your dander up and to see your cheeks become as red as your hair."

"I don't have red hair!" protested Daphne, for her hair was a sore point. The color had become more satisfactory as she had grown older, but there was still too much ginger in it for it to be called blonde.

"But you have. And the temper to go with it."

Daphne wanted to stamp her feet in rage, but knew that Caleb delighted in making her behave like a child. She composed her face into her coolest, most ladylike gaze, one she had practiced for long hours in front of her mirror. But Caleb only laughed harder.

"How fortunate. We are to be seated next to one another."

"Oh, no!" exclaimed Daphne without thinking. She had checked earlier to make sure that Caleb would not be sitting by her. Someone must have moved the place cards!

"What causes you to cry out? Have I stepped on your dress?" Caleb inquired, knowing full well what had prompted Daphne's outburst.

"Not at all," replied Daphne, setting her chin determinedly. Caleb Winters may sit beside her for as long as he liked, but she wouldn't speak to him. Young Reverend Mayberry was on her other side and he would receive all her attention.

The table before them was laid with silver, china and crystal, all reflecting the flickering lights of the crystal chandelier above them. At the center of the table were crystal dishes of hothouse grapes and the finest of early summer fruits. These alternated with dishes heaped with almonds.

The desserts were laid out at the end of the room, on another table. There were pyramids of macaroons in barley sugar, more pyramids of quartered oranges veiled with spun sugar. There were six kinds of layer cakes and as many kinds of pies. Baskets of flowers in all their brilliance surrounded the food. Daphne knew that at the end of the meal, ice cream in extraordinary shapes would be brought out as the *pièce de résistance*.

"You and your aunt have set a lovely table," the Reverend Horace Mayberry said sincerely. "I so look forward to my visits here, for not only are you and your aunt two of the finest Christian ladies in Pittsburgh, but you set the finest table as well."

His duty at an end, the reverend began to look at the dinner the footman behind him was piling on his plate. Daphne began to despair of conversation with him, for he was quite devoted to his food. At twenty-nine, he was already a portly man. Having no wife at home to see to the needs of his stomach, he looked particularly to his wealthy parishioners for satisfaction.

The meal went smoothly enough with lively conversation on all sides and an occasional word from Reverend Mayberry between courses. Politeness required Daphne to speak to Caleb, so she did so, but only briefly.

"You left so quickly after our little chat at the Point the other day that I had no opportunity to tell you how much I enjoyed our meeting."

"I should not have thought that you would bring that up, Mr. Winters. I should say that interview was best forgotten," replied Daphne.

"I assure you that I'll never forget it. There are certain moments that I cherish most particularly."

"And how do you find President Rutherford B. Hayes? Is he to your liking, now that you have had six months to observe him?"

"I imagine that you wish to change the subject."

"You may imagine what you will, but I wish you'd have the good grace to answer my question," snapped Daphne somewhat more sharply than she had intended to.

At last, dinner was at an end and the ladies gathered around the coffee urn in the small, pleasant front parlor and chatted. The conversation seemed dull after Daphne's lively struggles with Caleb during dinner. She responded mechanically to the small talk, turning over in her mind brilliant replies to Caleb's jibes.

Catherine Winters joined her and the two girls settled down on the settee.

"I never saw anything so funny as when you were talking to Mrs. Humphreyville," giggled Catherine. "She is a most formidable woman. She's been here practically since there were Indians in Pittsburgh."

"No wonder she looks like an old battle-axe," replied Daphne, sending them both into peals of laughter.

Suddenly Mrs. Humphreyville's emphatic voice boomed forth once more. "I, for one, cannot fathom your interest in this Bernhardt creature. In my time, we had real stars. Why, in '51, Jenny Lind came and sang at the Masonic Hall. Now, there was a singer! Like an angel in Paradise. The crowds were mad for her, tickets sold out days in advance. There was rioting on opening night. The poor woman was afraid to leave her dressing room. What a reception! What a voice! After someone of her caliber has shown you what singing can be, one cannot abide any other voice. I would never deign to hear such an inferior being as that French creature."

"She is not a singer, but an actress, ma'am," stated Daphne.

"Don't contradict Mrs. Humphreyville, Daphne," interposed Elspeth. "She is a respected authority on all cultural matters. It is largely due to her efforts that Pittsburgh has a cultural life at all and we all thank you most heartily, Alzina."

Her aunt's timely interference, while being somewhat humiliating to Daphne, saved her from a further scolding from the redoubtable Mrs. Humphreyville. The fact that Bernhardt was in fact an actress had nothing to do with the matter. Apparently, Mrs. Humphreyville must always be right.

Soon the gentlemen burst into the parlor, still involved in the heated argument they had begun in the dining room regarding the first term of Rutherford B. Hayes' presidency. They were bemoaning the loss of prosperity they all had enjoyed in the post-war boom economy of the late '60s and early '70s. That had ended quite abruptly with the collapse of Jay Cooke's banking house.

"The man is a fool!" exclaimed Jeb Slater as he entered the drawing room. "Good evening, ladies. We have just been discussing that rash young Andrew Carnegie. Just when all of us are pulling back because of the depression, he has the bad sense to begin building at Braddock's Fields. Of all the outlandish things!"

"Aye," agreed Colonel Foster. "These are rash plans."

"There are a dozen steel mills in Pittsburgh already," added James Frazier, who owned one of the largest of them. "How can he hope to compete with us while he pays off the tremendous debts he has incurred in building the plant?"

"That I can answer, gentlemen," drawled Caleb Winters. "He will undercut all of your prices because his plant will be the most modern of any in Pittsburgh. He is to use the new Bessemer process. Is labor cheap now? Of course. And materials are cheap as many men go out of business and sell their stock for next to nothing. This wretched depression will end, and if I had the ready cash, I, like Carnegie, would be building an empire and waiting for the tide to turn."

Jeb Slater had been rubbing his salt-and-pepper beard thoughtfully during Caleb's speech. "There may be sense in what you say, Caleb. That is a young man for you! An endless font of optimism and full of plans. We old-timers must be left behind by such men,¯ gentlemen. Yes, I don't doubt that you and Carnegie must understand each other very well, for you are of the same generation."

"Speak for yourself, Jeb, but I don't consider myself quite finished yet," replied James Frazier. "I'll give that young rascal a run for his money. Why I remember when he used to deliver telegrams to my office. It wasn't so long ago. The young may be optimistic, but they aren't wise and there lies the fault."

"Time will tell," sighed Jeb. "But I believe we may be boring the ladies. I think that I hear old Whitaker tuning up. I'd like to see some of you take a turn around the floor with our Pittsburgh belles. Shall we go in, Elspeth?" he smiled, offering his arm.

The parquet floor of the ballroom shone beneath the gaslights of the crystal chandelier and the ruby-colored glass wall sconces. The long windows were draped in deep maroon velvet, and the chairs lining the walls of the room were of matching maroon velvet accented with gold.

The dancing brought color to Daphne's cheeks and turned them as rosy as her dress. Even Catherine Winters began to glow. Daphne was sorry to have Caleb for a partner, although he danced well and looked handsome in his evening clothes. Everything seemed to have conspired to throw them together this evening, everything being her aunt and father and Caleb himself. Before the music had begun, she had watched Caleb push his sister toward Tad Billinghurst. Would Caleb ever stop pressing his suit? And did he truly believe that Tad was a serious suitor? Daphne sighed. The room was very warm and she was tense and tired at the same time. The room spun around and around. She saw only the lights and the flowers and Caleb's face bending over her. The music enveloped her like a cloud. Daphne breathed deeply, her breasts rising high above the low-cut bodice. The waist was so tight that it was difficult for her to breathe.

"You seem a bit faint, Daphne. Shall we go into the conservatory? You can catch your breath there."

Daphne merely nodded and allowed herself to be guided by Caleb to the cool, dark conservatory. She heard once again music from the ballroom and the tinkle and splash of the conservatory fountain. Caleb's voice reached her from what seemed far away.

"How lovely you are, Daphne," murmured Caleb softly, stroking her cheek. "We will be so happy together. Oh, give up your foolish objections! Say yes!"

Caleb leaned over her, his eyes devouring her face. Suddenly he was upon her, his lips pressing her mouth. Daphne gasped, struggling futilely against him. The greenery swam before her and the room spun around once, twice, before she slumped in Caleb's arms and fell to the floor in a swoon.

Chapter 6

Imagine me fainting! Just as though I were the heroine in a novel! What a fuss everyone made, even Aunt Elspeth, mused Daphne. Papa sent for the doctor, Caleb was embarrassed, all the ladies were in a tizzy. And all because my stays were too tight and I couldn't breathe. That should teach Caleb Winters to go around kissing young ladies who don't want to be kissed. Daphne giggled, glancing around at the other passengers on the streetcar.

The streetcar bell rang and Daphne got off and made her way through Bayardstown to the settlement house on Allegheny Street. Daphne often had heard her aunt speak of the old Schoenberger house and of the balls Elspeth had attended there in her youth. The house had long ago fallen on hard times, the streets around it turning into slums. As Daphne walked along busy Allegheny Street with its many cheap shops and street vendors, she felt an affection for the old house, standing proudly among its new

75

neighbors. The front of the old house was graced by a broad verandah. Wicker chairs were set about on the verandah, seeming to call out to passers-by to come up and chat.

The front door stood ajar, so Daphne walked right in, carrying her basket firmly. The front hall was dim, but she could make out several white marble statues. A fine mahogany staircase led to the upper regions of the house. The drawing room doors were shut. The place seemed empty. Daphne wondered what to do. It hardly seemed proper to wander through the house looking for someone. What should she do? Soon she heard someone walking rapidly on the floor above. Then the footsteps flew down the stairs and Daphne saw a small, dark-haired, pleasant-faced woman in her early thirties, dressed simply in a white blouse and black skirt with only a slight bustle. She was obviously the maid.

"Excuse me, would you please tell Miss Drummond that Miss Slater has come to call?" Daphne spoke to the maid.

"You could tell her yourself, if she weren't so busy. Oh, I see you're puzzled by my humor. I admit it's a bit queer. I am Lilleth Drummond. How do you do, Miss Slater?" The woman extended her hand, smiling engagingly.

"You?" said Daphne, automatically shaking the hand proffered to her.

"Yes. It's good to meet you at last, after hearing about you. Why don't we go straight in and I can show you around?" continued Miss Drummond, taking Daphne's arm and leading her down a corridor.

Daphne was too surprised by Miss Drummond's words and demeanor to do anything but follow. It seemed that Miss Drummond already knew of Daphne and had been expecting her, but how could that be? Daphne had told no one of her plans to visit the settlement house.

"We're so pleased that you've taken an interest in the nursery. We really do need your help. Ah, here we are!" cried Miss Drummond, throwing open a door. The scene was one of chaos. Small children in clean white pinafores were running around the room. Their younger brothers and sisters sat on cots against the walls, watching the activity in the room. There were several young women in charge. All activity momentarily ceased as Daphne and Miss Drummond entered the room. Then the children crowded around Miss Drummond. She smiled down fondly at them, listening to their babbling. Some shouted in broken English, but most spoke other languages.

"Children, children," shushed Miss Drummond, "you must all be quiet and meet this nice lady who has come to help us here at the settlement. This is Miss Slater. Say hello, please." A touching chorus of high-pitched voices cried, "Hello!"

Daphne smiled at the children and as she began to speak, the door opened and two young women entered.

The taller of the two, a fair-haired woman, said, "Miss Drummond, I've brought Miss Hillyer up. She was in the foyer an unconscionably long time."

"I didn't mind," replied the other woman softly. "I was admiring your beautiful statues. What a wonderful nursery! I'm sure I'll like it here."

"Why, my dear Miss Hillyer! How foolish of me. I mistook this other young lady for you in my haste. Well! Do excuse me, both of you. Kirsten Hoffstatter, you have been a godsend once again. Miss Hoffstatter, this is Miss Slater. Miss Slater, Miss Hillyer." Hands were shaken all around and smiles were exchanged. "Dear me! I assumed that you, Miss Slater, were Miss Hillyer! Forgive me, Miss Slater, but who *are* you?"

"Why, I can't exactly say who I am. Just a girl who's spent her whole life in Pittsburgh. But I can tell you why I came here. I've long admired your work and lately have felt that I should offer my help. I came today to see if I could be of any assistance."

"That was most kind of you, Miss Slater. I'm sure you can help us very much. Would you care to listen as I give my background talk on the history of this settlement nursery to Miss Hillyer?"

Daphne nodded and the two young women listened intently.

"The first summer that we had the settlement in Pittsburgh, we noticed that the children had no place to go during the day. The rooms in the tenements are dreadfully hot in summertime. The poor mites began to come to us because this old house is so cool. Soon the house was overrun with children, so we assigned Miss Hoffstatter to supervise them and we set aside these rooms as the nursery. Now the nursery is in operation winter and summer. Working mothers now have a safe place to leave their children. Miss Hoffstatter and I find that we need help. Both you, Miss Hillyer, and you, Miss Slater, are a gift from heaven. I'll leave you, Miss Hillyer, to get acquainted with the children. Miss Slater, would you please come with me?"

Soon Daphne found herself in a pleasant drawing room on the ground floor. Miss Drummond had deposited her there promising to return shortly. Miss Hoffstatter had vanished to another part of the house with a look of being very busy. Daphne was glad to have a few moments to herself, for she'd been in a constant whirl ever since meeting Miss Drummond.

Daphne looked about the room. It was set up as an office, Daphne assumed for Miss Drummond. A large desk stood against one wall, its surface scattered with papers. Above it was a bookshelf of worn volumes, including books by Tolstoy and the founders of the English settlement house movement. A couple of worn chairs, a small tea table and another bookcase completed the furnishings. Photographs of ancient ruins adorned the walls. It was a room that revealed much about its occupant. Daphne could tell that behind Miss Drummond's distracted air lay a serious and thoughtful woman who was as much occupied with the cares of the world as with philosophy.

"Now, Miss Slater! Do let me apologize again for this morning's mix up," said Lilleth Drummond as she bustled in. "We are not always so confused here. Please tell me what sort of work you would like to do for us."

"Oh, Miss Drummond. I really can't say. I'd never been to Bayardstown until last week, and I was so strongly affected by the misery there that I felt I should do something to improve the lives of these poor people. I knew of your work and hoped that you could provide me with direction and employment. I have led such a narrow life. Oh, I've been educated, but I feel that I know next to nothing about the world. I want to do something for others."

"I see. I fully understand, Miss Slater. There is a

great deal you can do here, believe me, and you'll be most appreciated."

"But how can I help? I've had some training in art and music and literature, but I know nothing practical, nothing useful."

"Those things are useful. People need the arts just as they need food. We have a great many lectures in our drawing room and they are all well attended. There is such a thirst for learning here! Your knowledge of America and American ways is craved by the immigrants who come here."

"Heddie works as a maid for my family and I heard about you from her. She takes English lessons here."

"Heddie?"

"Oh, her real name is Hedwig, Hedwig Bronislavski, but I call her Heddie."

"Yes, I know the family. Heddie, as you call her, is a good girl. I am so relieved that she has found work, for she was nearly desperate. In these hard times so many girls turn to evil ways out of sheer desperation. The family's condition is a precarious one," continued Miss Drummond sadly. "Perhaps we can do something for them."

"I do hope so," Daphne said earnestly. "Heddie is a most determined girl. Why, she simply refused to leave our house until she had work. She even stood up to Cook and Hawkins, which I wouldn't have had the courage for at her age."

"Of course," Miss Drummond continued about the settlement house, "we have a great many activities here other than lectures and English lessons and the nursery. We have a workingmen's association, which strives to create better conditions for workingmen in Pittsburgh. Fair wages, hours and a certain amount of security. Then there is a similar association for workingwomen. Basically, we try to be good neighbors and give help where it is needed. There's a great deal to be done in Bayardstown, and in all of Pittsburgh. Sanitary conditions are not what they ought to be and surely contribute to the high death rate here. And then there is child labor, which is such an abomination," concluded Miss Drummond with special feeling. "So you see, there are many things going on. I have the impression that you like young people. Am I right, Miss Slater?"

"Why, yes," answered Daphne.

"I think you would enjoy teaching an after-school class in English." Miss Drummond went on to tell Daphne something about her pupils and the methods used for teaching English. Daphne felt a thrill of excitement at the idea of being a teacher. It was almost like her fantasy of being a missionary in Africa except that it was not a fantasy at all. And Miss Drummond seemed to understand everything about her, although Daphne had hardly told her anything at all. Daphne was in awe of the wisdom and charm of this great lady.

A schedule was established for Daphne and the young teacher prepared to leave Miss Drummond's office. "This has been the most fascinating interview. I feel positively inspired and I will do my very best," Daphne promised as she took her leave. Shutting the door behind her, she had a glimpse of Miss Drummond already hard at work at her papers, the very picture of diligence. She wandered down the hallway and suddenly found herself face to face with the man from the woods.

"You!" cried Daphne. The two stared at one another in mutual surprise for a moment before Daphne was able to collect herself sufficiently to continue. "I should think you've bothered me enough with that letter. You needn't follow me as well. Don't think I'm frightened of you because I'm not."

"Miss Slater, I haven't followed you or written to you. What are you talking about? Besides, I live here. So it appears you have been following me."

"What? Here at the settlement house?" Daphne wondered whether she ought to believe the man.

"Come now, we have gotten off on the wrong foot. Allow me to present myself: Rene LeBrun." He bowed mockingly and took Daphne's hand, bringing it up to his lips. She snatched it away.

"Rene LeBrun," repeated Daphne. "But I thought you were a labor organizer."

"I'm not exactly an organizer, merely a laborer who wants to help his coworkers. But you haven't told me what letter you're referring to and what it has to do with me."

"I received a letter in the post that threatened me with harm and was signed by the Knights of Labor. It seemed an obvious attempt to frighten me."

"Do you still have the letter?"

"No, I burned it immediately."

"Can you remember exactly what it said?" Rene seemed very concerned.

"I really can't trouble myself to recall the note, though it probably was typical, as well as crude."

"You'd best recall it. Have some regard for your own safety!" exclaimed Rene harshly. "Whoever sent you that note meant you harm." His eyes were troubled and passionate. Daphne could not bear his intense gaze for more than a moment. She lowered her eyes and replied obediently, "The letter said to be careful and not to cross the Knights of Labor, or else. That's all it said, but it was all misspelled."

"Miss Slater," Rene spoke slowly and deliberately, "there are some desperate men in this city. Please be careful. Too little fear can be as dangerous as too much."

Suddenly Daphne looked up and accused, "You did have something to do with that letter! You are in league with them. You didn't seem the sort who'd threaten a woman, but now I see how wrong I was."

"You mistake my meaning, Miss Slater," said Rene quietly.

"I'll leave you in no doubt of mine, Mr. LeBrun. I hope that we'll never have occasion to meet again and further, I'll report to Miss Drummond what I have found out about you. I don't think she'll allow you to stay on once she knows you for what you are," Daphne finished heatedly.

"Report me to whom you like. I care nothing for the baseless accusations of a schoolgirl," replied Rene, his flashing grey eyes belying his calm, careless words.

"What an insufferable man you are!" cried Daphne, rushing from the room.

Out in the foyer Daphne nearly collided with a sobbing form sitting on the bottom step of the staircase. Twilight had descended and the gas lamps had not yet been lit, so it took a moment for Daphne to realize that it was Heddie.

"Oh, miss," cried Heddie, flinging herself into Daphne's arms. "It's Mama!"

"What's happened, Heddie?"

Poor Heddie was crying too hard to make herself

understood. Daphne held her and let her give way to her grief. She feared that Mrs. Bronislavski was dead. Finally, Heddie composed herself and said, "Mama's worse. The doctor won't come without money. I come for Miss Drummond, but she ain't in and I'm so frightened."

"We'll go and get the doctor. I have money, Heddie. But we must hurry."

"Oh yes, miss. Thank you!" Heddie cried, a smile lighting her pale face. And with that, the two young women rushed out into the night.

Chapter 7

The miners huddled together in the predawn light, standing at the entrance to the mine shaft, most barely awake. They were waiting for the elevator that would take them four hundred feet underground to the coal face. There they would dig for seven hours almost without rest. The men pulled their jackets more tightly around themselves to ward off the early morning chill.

Rene LeBrun stood slightly to one side regarding the bleak, grey ground around the mine shaft with its towering slag heaps and hastily built breaker sheds and outbuildings. Rene took a deep breath of the fresh morning air, preparing himself for the descent into the damp darkness where the atmosphere was thick with coal dust and each moment was fraught with the possibility of disaster.

The steam-powered elevator arrived and the men on the night shift stumbled out of the small car, blinking in the dawn light. Their faces were black with coal dust. The men of the day shift boarded the elevator. The two groups did not speak.

As Rene entered the elevator, a miner he had never seen before stood in front of him, blocking his way and looking deeply into his eyes. The man's face was haggard and drawn, his eyes black-rimmed with coal dust.

"It'll be bad luck for you if you go down. And for your buddy," threatened the stranger in a hoarse voice.

Rene stared at the man. "Let me pass."

The man moved reluctantly to one side and stood staring at Rene. Rene entered and the elevator began its descent.

Miners are a superstitious lot, thought Rene, trying to brush aside the miner's ominous warning. He decided to forget what the man had said.

Rene stepped from the elevator and walked along the tunnel that led to the part of the coal face he was working. All around him miners hurried to their work, bending low to avoid hitting their heads against the low ceilings. The ground was uneven and, in places, Rene found himself up to his ankles in coal-blackened water. In the darkness around him, Rene could see pinpoints of moving light as miners went to their places. The candles that were set into small lamps in their hats flickered as the miners went about their work. After almost half an hour's walk, Rene reached his position and greeted Angelo, the laborer assigned to help him. The two men then set to work.

Soon Rene's pick was working rhythmically breaking up the coal. Finally, he took up his shovel and scooped the loosened coal out of the rock face and threw it backwards over his shoulder into a waiting cart. Angelo piled the coal into the cart more securely and pushed the cart out into the corridor. From there it would be taken up to the shaft by a pit pony. Then Angelo returned and placed another wagon behind Rene to catch the next shovelfuls of glistening black lumps.

As Angelo worked he marveled at the way Rene wielded his pick and shovel. It seemed to him that Rene was more machine than man at these times. Kneeling in a tiny space, he moved mountains of coal each day, and never seemed to tire.

Rene broke into Angelo's reverie. "Hungry? We can take a few minutes for lunch now."

The two men sat down against one of the walls and opened their lunch cases. They ate their bread and drippings hungrily and gulped the cold tea they had brought with them.

"I heard there was a bit of trouble with last night's shift. A rock slide," Rene said quietly.

Angelo's eyes grew round with fear and he murmured a silent prayer, but nothing further was said on the subject.

An hour later, a pit pony came down the tunnel and the men moved back to let the animal pass. It strained beneath its load of coal. Suddenly the pony stopped in its tracks and, quivering all over, gave a whinny of fear. The driver who had been leading the pony turned around.

"Get on with you, you wretched animal!" he cried, tugging at the animal's bridle, but the horse would not move. The man took up his whip and, cursing, began to beat the pony. Still, it would not move.

Rene grabbed the man's arm. "Stop. He's just

frightened. Most likely a mouse or something ran in front of him."

At last the man stopped pulling at the pony's bridle and the animal moved on.

Angelo whispered, "When an animal does that it gives me a spooky feeling." His voice sounded strained.

The men moved in silence back to their jobs and once more Rene threw himself into his work. He was tense, now every muscle prepared to feel the slightest tremor. He listened for a creaking sound from the beams supporting the ceiling. Soon enough, he heard the dreaded creaking. He threw down his pick and looked around for Angelo. At that instant a great rumbling began and the world seemed to shift about the two men.

At the plaintive sound of the mine whistle, Caleb leapt from his desk and ran to the window. In the yard below men were running frantically. Caleb's face assumed a determined, steely expression.

If any of them are alive, we'll get them out, he thought to himself, clenching his fists.

Caleb made his way through the crowded yard to the mine shaft, where the miners' wives already were beginning to file into the yard to stand in silent vigil. Caleb felt their eyes upon him and avoided looking at the women. He spotted Casey, the yard foreman, and hailed him. "How many dead?"

"We're not sure. LeBrun and Burfoot were working down there and they haven't come up. Not much chance of their coming up now, either."

"Why?"

"Traces of monoxide gas. The men refuse to go

down and dig them out. Say it's too dangerous. Just as well, those two were troublemakers."

"I hear you talk like that again, Casey, and that'll be the end of you," hissed Caleb. "We don't consign men to death. And I won't have men refusing to go down in the mines. I'll show them."

Caleb turned on his heel and strode purposefully to the elevator shaft, the men parting to let him through.

Turning to the miners, Caleb said, "I wouldn't ask you men to do anything I wouldn't do myself. I hear some of you think it's not safe down there. That may be so, but there's no excuse for not trying to save those trapped men. At this very moment, they are praying that we will save them before they run out of air. They'd do whatever they could for you. Now let's go find them."

Without a backward glance, Caleb turned and stepped into the elevator and many of the men followed.

The first sounds Rene heard after the rumble of falling rocks and roof had subsided were Angelo's moans. The tunnel was in total darkness, for their candles had gone out. Rene stretched cautiously, grateful to realize that he had broken no bones.

"Angelo?" called Rene. "It's all right. I'm here. I'm coming to get you."

He heard a soft moan.

A voice nearby startled him. "So, you made it, too, you old son of a gun." It was Asa Burfoot, a long-time laborer. "Let's light the candles and see what we've got here." Asa, too, was unhurt.

The mine roof had collapsed, blocking the only

exit from the mine. Angelo was trapped beneath a fall of rubble, a huge rock pinning his legs. His young face was contorted with pain.

"We've got to start digging from this side and hope that they begin from the other side right away. We'll· be out of air in no time in this rat hole," said Rene. "But let's try to get Angelo out before we dig."

The two men began wielding their picks, hoping all the while that the ceiling wouldn't give way again. After removing some of the smaller boulders that trapped Angelo, the men realized that it was pointless for them to attempt to move the large one. It was just too heavy. Without a word, they concentrated their efforts at a likely looking point in the solidly packed wall of stones, their faces set in lines of grim determination.

The air steadily became more noxious. The men gasped for breath as they strained to work more quickly. Angelo slipped in and out of consciousness.

The sudden clanking of picks on the other side of the rubble brought immediate hope. Suddenly a pick from the other side emerged through the rubble and men on both sides shouted for joy. Air began to flow through the room.

Rene went to the new opening and shouted, "One of the men in here is trapped under a boulder about two feet to the left of this hole, so watch your picks. Two of us are digging out from this end."

The men set to with their picks once more. All were fearful of another cave-in. The ceiling was still unstable and could collapse at any time.

The hole in the wall of rock became larger. A wooden support to hold up the ceiling was passed through. Then water was passed through.

The wall began to weaken dangerously. On the other side, Caleb pushed on fiercely. His costly suit was covered with coal dust, the jacket ripped at the seams from the pressure of his muscles working the pick. He continued digging, heedless of danger, but the others hung back in fear. With the miner's sixth sense, they could feel the walls weakening. Caleb's hands were raw, but he dug on in a fury.

The wooden supports holding up the ceiling creaked ominously.

"Put up more supports on your side," shouted Rene to Caleb through the wall. "That ceiling's about to come down on you. I can feel it."

"Don't worry about us. The ceiling will hold until we can get you out. Dig, boys, dig! You men over there, put up more supports."

The fight against time continued, but each side knew that they could only lose the battle. The men in the tunnel could see that the mine walls and ceiling were becoming more and more unstable. They were bracing themselves for another cave-in. Once that happened, assuming they were not killed in the crash, all hopes for the men on the other side would be lost. It was lucky enough that they had lived through the first collapse.

Rene and Asa looked anxiously at Angelo. He was beginning to become delirious. He moaned and tossed his head, talking to himself in Italian. They feared that he would not live long enough to be dug out of their horrible trap.

Two beams gave way simultaneously and the ceiling came down on the three embattled men once again. There was the sound of falling rock and then silence.

"We're still in here," cried Asa. "If you're alive out there, get us out!"

"By the grace of God, we are," replied Caleb. "Are you all safe?"

"Angelo's dead, God help him. Rene's knocked out, but I think he's alive. I'm fine, but stuck between a rock and a hard place. Now, stop gabbing and get us out." Asa's good humor cheered the men and spurred them on.

Luck was with them. The second rock fall had loosened the wall of stones separating the two groups of men. Caleb and his men dug away rapidly at the loose stones, heaping them into piles behind them. The ceiling was still unstable and there was always the danger of released gases.

Asa was freed first and was helped to the surface, protesting that he should help with the digging. Rene was taken out on a stretcher a few minutes later. For a while, it seemed that Angelo's body would stay in the mine, but Caleb refused to allow this. Finally, his body was brought to the surface.

The grateful eyes of women and children greeted Caleb when he came to the surface. He looked at them without fear for he had done his best to rescue his men. But one woman, Angelo's mother, looked steadfastly at him with hatred and anguish.

Chapter 8

Sunlight sparkled over the country meadow, lighting the long grasses, the newly opened wildflowers and the young girl who stood in their midst as though she were one of them. But Daphne's thoughts were not on the bright, sunny day, the hum of the bees or the dancing of the flowers. She felt herself still in the dank tenement rooms of the Bronislavskis, watching over Heddie's poor, tired mother as she hovered near death.

Daphne's vigil had been a long one, but finally the doctor had saved Mrs. Bronislavski. When Daphne had left the house late that night, the exhausted woman was asleep at last. Death had come much too close and had left its mark on Daphne.

My life has been completely turned upside down in the past week, Daphne mused. I used to be such a dreamer, but now I have no time for dreams. What a whirl my life is! And now I am a teacher!

Daphne sat down amidst the daisies to contem-

plate further this blissful state. She had given her first
lesson on Friday and had loved it. The children were
so good, the schoolroom so exactly like what a schoolroom should be, Miss Drummond such a marvel.

Thirty children of many different nationalities
had sat on rows of benches before her. Their eyes had
fastened upon her eagerly, for she was the lady who
would teach them English and start them on the road
to becoming real Americans. Shaking from nervousness, Daphne began to talk to the children and soon
they were repeating her words. It amazed Daphne
how fresh and eager the children had been during the
long day in school. She was ashamed to recall how re-
luctant she had been to do her lessons when she was
a child.

It's not that I'm such a wonderful teacher, but
that I have such talented pupils. They want so much
to learn, Daphne thought. She could barely wait for
Monday to come so that she could go to the settlement house once more and help the children.

Daphne stood up, brushing the grass from her
pink gingham dress and tying the matching bonnet
more firmly under her chin. She had spent too many
days washing her face with lemon juice in an effort to
rid herself of freckles to be careless of her skin. She
always wore bonnets in the summer.

She could hear the music of the Allegheny River
beckoning to her from just beyond a glade of elms
and birches. She wandered toward the sound, running
her hands through the long grasses as she walked.
Once inside the glade, the light dappled as sunlight
struggled to find its way between the new leaves.
Daphne loosened the strings of her bonnet and threw

it back from her head so that it rested against her shoulders. Her hair blew loosely.

Suddenly there was a break in the trees ahead and she saw the river. It was a dazzling blue and the current was quite swift. Daphne could see Wainwright Island a few feet away. She recalled picnics there in her childhood and felt a warm nostalgia for the place.

The island looked so near, so wild and so beautiful that Daphne stepped closer to the river's edge in order to get a better look at it. Perhaps it was the dry earth around the river, for there had been no rain in over a week. Perhaps it was Daphne's preoccupation with her thoughts, or maybe it was her flimsy kid slippers. Perhaps it was all of these things. Suddenly, the earth beneath her crumbled and Daphne, who had been leaning over the water peering at the island, fell into the river and was swept away from shore into the rapid current.

The cold water and the surprise of the fall took her breath away. She began to swim, but her heavy skirts encumbered her legs and her bonnet string was almost strangling her. Daphne was a good swimmer, but she found herself unable to catch her breath. Traveling farther and faster downriver, she began to scream, although she knew there was no one to hear her. Just as the waters were closing over her head, she believed she saw someone leap into the river.

Her imagination was conjuring up a rescuer, she realized in despair. But no! There really was a strong arm around her, and then another, and soon she was being lifted up. She strained to hold her head above water as her rescuer swam with one arm, the other holding her tightly. Soon they were clear of the current and at last he deposited her on the bank. With strength born of relief, Daphne scrambled over the bank onto safe ground. She gasped for air, steadying herself. Only when she felt truly safe did she look up, recognizing her rescuer with shock. It was Rene! Rene, the scoundrel! She blushed at the mere thought. Never again could she call Rene a scoundrel. He had saved her from drowning.

Having caught his breath, he spoke. "Calm yourself, Miss Slater. You must rest for a moment. Lie back and relax."

Daphne lay back meekly and allowed Rene to put his dry coat over her soaking dress. Despite the warmth of the day, both were shivering.

"How did you fall into the river?" Rene asked. Daphne explained.

Rene set about making a fire to warm them both. Soon it was crackling merrily before them. Daphne stretched out her numb hands.

"Excuse me for a moment, Miss Slater. I left a few of my things in those bushes over there where I was reading. I want to get them," said Rene. He returned shortly, carrying a book and a small parcel. Terribly embarrassed, Daphne suddenly realized that she had not thanked Rene for rescuing her. What was the matter with her? She began shyly, unable to meet his eyes.

"Mr. LeBrun, I . . . I realize that I accused you yesterday of having written that terrible letter. I shouldn't have done so. You told me that you hadn't written it and I ought to have taken your word. You are obviously a gentleman and it was ill-mannered of me to question you." She glanced up at him quickly to see how he was taking this, but his face registered only sincerity. No, this was no scoundrel. "And I want to thank you for saving me just now. I owe you my life, in fact."

"I'm glad to have been here when I was needed, that's all, Miss Slater," he replied gravely. "Not for the world would I see you hurt. Not for the world," he finished gently.

Daphne could find no answer to the feeling in Rene's voice. At least no answer that she could speak. But her heart made its own reply, surprising her as much as his declaration had done.

"Why, you are soaking wet!" Daphne cried.

"I did just take a swim," replied Rene.

For some reason, this struck them both as terribly funny and they began to laugh. Soon all the barriers between them were gone and they began talking of everything. Never had Daphne met someone who spoke what she herself felt quite as well as Rene did.

Daphne and Rene leaned against the warm stones a few yards from the bank of the river, the fire warming their feet. Daphne's bonnet lay drying beside her, as did their shoes. There was something inexpressibly cozy about their talk.

"Do you like poetry, Daphne? I've been reading Whitman's poems from *Leaves of Grass*. Would you like to hear some?"

Daphne nodded and soon the two heads were bent over one thin volume of poems. Rene's sonorous voice reverberated in the stillness. Daphne felt her soul stirred to its very depths. Rene's voice was soothing and having him so near thrilled her. At last the poem came to an end and he shut the book.

Rene turned his grey eyes toward Daphne. She made a lovely picture, smiling gently in the sun, her reddish-blonde hair loose and curly, the simple pink dress charming. Rene caught his breath at the loveliness of her.

Daphne was looking at Rene just as intently. He was so fine, so handsome. His dark hair curled back from his face. His eyes held such depth of feeling. Suddenly, though not a word was spoken, they seemed to know everything about one another, all at once. And then, inevitably, Daphne found herself in Rene's arms, his mouth soft and then firm against hers. She gasped, returning his kiss.

Rene tenderly kissed her cheeks, her eyelids, her forehead. Daphne felt too elated for speech. She rested in his arms, hiding her face against his neck, giving herself to him.

She nearly had lost all caution when Rene shook himself, holding her at arm's length. "Daphne, what is this madness that has come over us? I, I can't explain how I came to . . . ."

"Oh, Rene. I don't know what it is, but it is not madness. Rene . . . ."

"Don't say anything you may regret later. We are too different, Daphne. Our lives are so different. We can't go on. We must stop this while we can."

Daphne was too stunned to reply. How could Rene speak of walling up the feelings that now were flooding all her senses? She could as little do that as she could stop her heart from beating. She knew that she loved him. She must be with him.

"We must be strong and leave this place, Daphne. Think, think what it will mean if we continue!"

"It will mean that we always will be together," said Daphne dreamily.

"But at what cost? We come from two different worlds. I can't live in yours and I fear that you'd be unhappy in mine. You will be an outcast if you . . ." Rene could not bring himself to say the word love, fearing that the simple word would release all the feelings he strove to suppress.

Daphne was shocked. She had begun to love him, yet he was telling her that their love could not be. Perhaps he did not love her and had only felt some low urgings of the flesh. Was that it? Revulsion swept over her. He did not love her. He felt none of what she felt. Daphne was ill, heartsick, and wanted only to hurt Rene, to hurt him as he had hurt her.

"I must leave," she announced coldly. "My fiancé is waiting for me."

"Your what?"

"You know that I am to be married to Caleb Winters," said Daphne as calmly as she could.

"Caleb Winters?"

"Must you repeat everything like a parrot? Good day," said Daphne, turning away to put on her shoes and bonnet.

Rene sat in stunned silence.

"Thank you for troubling to save my life. It was most kind." Without looking at him she walked rapidly away, a searing pain tearing at her.

What would she have thought had she seen Rene staring into the ashes of the fire after she left, finally removing one page from the volume of poems and adding it to the blaze? Would she have regretted her words if she had seen Rene pull the burning page from the fire, sadly folding what was left of it and placing it gently in his pocket?

Chapter 9

Daphne hurried upstairs to change her gown before her aunt saw her. The gown was still wet and mud clung to her skirt. Once in her room, Daphne ripped off the dress and threw it to the floor. She would give it away. She never wanted to be reminded of this afternoon and its humiliations. After changing into dry clothes, Daphne sat at her dressing table, brushing out her tangled hair. She pulled viciously at it.

Suddenly Daphne put her head down on her arms and gave way to her grief. She could not understand why Rene had treated her so cruelly.

"I was a fool-to give my heart so easily. How could I have been so mistaken? Oh, Rene, Rene," Daphne sighed, her eyes filling again.

Much later, she washed her face and, calmer now, went downstairs to the library, where she knew she would not be disturbed.

The house was silent. Midafternoon on a Sunday was a quiet time in the Slater household. Daphne's father and aunt were usually out making calls and the servants had a half-day off. The library was dark and empty. Daphne selected a volume from one of the mahogany shelves that lined the walls and went to the window seat. Sitting on the ledge and pulling the red velvet draperies around her, she was instantly lost from view. From childhood, this had been Daphne's favorite place to read. The bay window curved around enclosing her as though she were inside a bubble. The shrubbery growing against the window protected her from the prying eyes of anyone outside.

She glanced at the title of the book she was holding, and she gasped. It was *Leaves of Grass* by Walt Whitman. She looked through the book to find the poem she and Rene had read together. It seemed that if she could find the poem and read it again, she would hear Rene's voice and feel his lips on hers once more. She held the book to her breast and thought, I am a coward. I must give him up. He doesn't love me. And yet I can't give him up. But I must. I must put this book away. I must force msyelf to think of something else.

Just as Daphne was about to pull back the curtains so that she could return the book to its place, she heard the library door open. She kept silent, not wanting to be discovered. Maybe whoever it was would leave quickly. She didn't want to talk to anyone.

"We can talk privately in here." It was her father's voice.

Oh, dear, he has a guest. I can't come out, now. Maybe they won't be long, thought Daphne.

"Daphne is out. There is no danger of her overhearing us," Jeb continued.

"You don't keep a very close rein on her." The speaker's voice chilled Daphne. It was Caleb Winters.

"Daphne needs freedom. She is still young and needs to be given her head, rather like an unbroken horse. Once the two of you are married, you can treat her differently, of course, but I wouldn't advise it."

"I begin to doubt that she and I ever will marry. She is unwilling."

"It's just youth, my boy. High spirits. You know how children are. They like the freedom to say no," Jeb chuckled. "I was that way myself. The best way to get her consent is to leave her to herself for a while. Don't pressure her. I think we've been wrong in trying to force her. She's stubborn, like her father."

"A young woman shouldn't be so self-willed. Catherine was not raised to have such a high regard for her own opinion."

"Catherine is a fine girl, don't misunderstand me, Caleb, but she doesn't have Daphne's spirit. I know that Daphne will come to love you, or I wouldn't encourage the match. She's still a little young to marry. Give her time."

"I can't share your optimism, but I have the stronger will and am determined to win our contest whether she believes it or not. I shall marry her."

"Think of the prosperity it will bring. I wish you and Daphne happiness. Shall we drink to it?" suggested Jeb Slater. Daphne heard the clink of glass goblets as they toasted her downfall.

"You must have asked me here for some other reason than to talk about Daphne, Jeb," said Caleb. Something in his tone indicated to Daphne that he had no real respect for her father.

"Now, Caleb, what else could I want to speak of?" answered Jeb with a short, nervous laugh.

"Money. Or your lack of it," responded Caleb harshly. "You've been speculating again, haven't you?"

"Not this time. I no longer have the spirit for speculation. I need a loan. That's the plain truth of it. I need money to keep up the house. Daphne and Elspeth must never suspect what I have done. The business brings in nothing. And even if it did, my creditors would get every cent of it. Caleb, I need ten thousand dollars for the rest of the year."

"I would as soon give you money as I would give a drunkard a drink. You would gamble it all away."

"You are unfair, Caleb. I never should have admitted to you how deeply in debt I was. If only this depression would end. If only I had news of that new vein of iron."

"Life is a series of ifs for you, Jeb. Well, I can't finance them any longer. At least not until we have a common tie. Once I marry Daphne, my purse will be yours. Until then, I can help you no more."

"I won't press you for the money, Caleb," sighed Jeb in a defeated voice. "Perhaps you'd like to buy a share of one of my investments instead?"

"I think not. Your investments never turn out. You are rash, Jeb. You took a solid business and ran it into the ground. All the capital that should have gone into the business was poured into foolish new enterprises. You are in over your head, Jeb. You know you need me to help you out."

There was a silence in the room as the two men matched wits. Jeb walked to the fire and poked it, stalling for time. He gazed forlornly into the flames, recalling his lost fortune. At first speculation had seemed a sure way to make more money. Later, as his schemes failed, he invested more and more heavily in an attempt to recoup his losses. He sighed deeply.

"You must do as I say," Caleb ordered. "You are too deeply in debt to have any real choice, and you know it."

"What is it you want of me, Caleb?" asked Jeb flatly. "Does it have to do with Daphne?"

"No," replied Caleb scornfully, "it has nothing to do with her. You can't control your daughter any better than you can control your money. I'll deal with Daphne myself, and successfully.

"This other matter is of more importance. It concerns business. I want to make certain arrangements with you."

"My business is in ruins."

"But that is not known to anyone except the two of us. You give the impression of a successful man.

"I want you to join me in creating a monopoly on iron and coal in Pittsburgh. It is true that we don't have the resources to build a steel mill, but we can bring the steel men to their knees: You and I can control the raw materials.

"Together we'll undercut the prices of our competitors and ruin their businesses. Then we'll buy them out. I have the support of a bank, so we'll be financed well enough to accomplish this. But I want you to gain control of the iron. For me to do both at once would be too obvious. It will make you a rich man, Jeb."

"You want us to form a monopoly?" Jeb was taken aback.

"You speak that word as though you hate it."

"I do. Such business practices are unfair."

Caleb's laughter rang out. "I see that you are low enough to sell your daughter, but not so low as to sell your principles."

"I have fallen low indeed if I can be insulted in my own home. But I suppose I must bear it. You are right, of course. I have no choice. Yes, I must do as you tell me," Jeb whispered hoarsely.

"You won't regret it. You'll make your fortune again. We'll own Pittsburgh! Carnegie will be nothing!"

Daphne was too heartsick to listen any longer. Why couldn't her father give up the house and settle with his creditors, leaving himself poor but free . . . free of dishonor and free of Caleb Winters?

She became vaguely aware that the tone of their conversation had changed and that they seemed friendly once again.

"Yes, yes," her father agreed, "it will all work if only we can be rid of those damn unions. Oh, they may not seem like much now, but give them a few years and they'll own us. We must make certain that they never gain a following here in Pittsburgh, or our chance of making a lot of money is lost. Your plans depend on keeping wages low."

"No union will succeed here," Caleb said firmly. "For one thing, the workers have nothing in common. They come from too many different parts of the world to feel a common bond. A few troublemakers are causing all this union talk. The men themselves don't want anything until they are told what they want.

"I have a plan to get rid of them. Remove the top men, the labor organizers, and the whole movement will wither."

"But how can you remove the organizers if you don't know who they are?" asked Jeb.

"I have spies in the unions. They're ready to tell any lie at my bidding. The most dangerous of the unions is the Knights of Labor. If we destroy them, the rest will disappear as well.

"There is one special organizer in Pittsburgh. If we can stop that man, we will have crushed the union movement. I'm laying my traps and waiting for him to fall in."

"Who is that?"

"Rene LeBrun is his name," answered Caleb, hatred filling his voice. Daphne's heart sank. "I have an informer in his group. He is closely allied to the Knights of Labor and runs some sort of club at a settlement house in Bayardstown. My man is willing to testify that LeBrun has been plotting against the bosses, encouraging the men to form a violent rebellion. When the time is ripe, a bomb will go off and Rene LeBrun will be arrested for setting it. He will be tried and hanged, and that will be the end of the labor movement in Pittsburgh."

"Harsh measures," Jeb murmured. Caleb did not reply.

The two men left the room, slamming the door behind them. For a few seconds after they left, Daphne could hear their footsteps reverberating in the marble corridor. Only then did she realize that she had hardly been breathing at all.

Chapter 10

In her nightmare, Daphne struggled through the thick mists, desperately trying to push them aside. Something was horribly wrong. She could see nothing in front of her. She was afraid, but could not call out for help.

Suddenly the fog cleared and Daphne found herself in the middle of a square filled with people. It was noon, a bright day. In the center of the square stood a gallows. Everyone turned to stare at her as though they all had been waiting for her arrival. Despite the masses of people, complete silence reigned. The crowd parted and Daphne walked towards the gallows.

Rene, Caleb and her father appeared on the stage. By her side, Aunt Elspeth appeared and grabbed Daphne by the arm. She hissed, "It's all your fault. You are evil." Daphne recoiled, trying to pull away. She tried to defend herself, but she could make no sounds.

117

Caleb caught sight of Daphne and stared at her, grinning. His eyes drew her toward the platform. How I hate him, thought Daphne, but he draws me to him like a magnet. She tried to take her eyes off Caleb to look at her father and Rene, but she could not. Finally, she reached the platform and stopped.

Caleb's voice thundered. "Which one shall die? Your father or your lover? You must choose. One can go free but one must die."

"Please, Caleb, I'll do anything, but not that. I can't choose."

"You must choose or they both will die."

Executioners appeared on the platform and began to lead Rene and her father toward two nooses. The nooses were placed around their necks. Rene bore it stoically, his face like stone, but his eyes stared at her with passionate love and longing. Her father looked around wildly, a broken man, close to tears.

"Choose," demanded Caleb.

"Choose, choose," chanted the crowd.

"No! No!" screamed Daphne. Her cries awakened her. Her nightgown clung to her skin, glued by cold perspiration. Daphne could not quite believe it had been a dream. It all seemed so real. She could still see her father's stricken face and Rene's, and hear Caleb's laughter.

Daphne rose from her bed and rushed to the washstand, stripping off her nightgown on the way. She then washed herself in cold water, hoping the water would wipe the nightmare from her memory.

She slipped on a simple gown, a sprigged white muslin with a blue and lilac forget-me-not pattern. The neckline was rounded and the sleeves were short and puffed. It was not a terribly stylish dress, but it was perfect for a hot summer day.

Daphne peered at her reflection in the mirror and began to pin up her hair. The night's fears did not show on her smooth, unlined face. Daphne pulled her luxuriant reddish hair up on top of her head and piled it into a bun at the crown. Before she secured it with pins, she loosened several strands of hair about her face.

The pale dawn light in which Daphne had awakened was swiftly turning to bright sunshine. The birds had long since stopped their early morning serenade and were going about their business. The day was already old to them. Daphne sat by her window and looked out at the river. Barges filled with vegetables were arriving from the farms upriver. Other barges, laden with minerals, some from her father's mines near Lake Erie, made their slow, majestic way along the river. Daphne often had imagined Pittsburgh as a large beast that required constant feeding. The city was more real to her than most of the people she knew. Daphne supposed that being an only child had made her so fanciful.

Dreams had always been important to Daphne because they were usually so pleasant. It was like leading a second life. She usually didn't think that they had any relation to real life, but the dream that had awakened her this morning was different. It seemed to be a warning. She had to tell Rene that his life was in danger, even though that might mean financial ruin for her father if Caleb were to discover what she had done. Daphne had made her choice.

A faint knock at the door interrupted Daphne's reverie. Heddie entered the room, her eyes red-rimmed. The eyes of the two girls met and Daphne's eyes too filled with tears at the sight of Heddie's distress.

"Mama's worse, Miss Daphne. She's very sick. The doctor don't think . . ." Her words trailed off in sobs. "I come to ask if you could stay with her today and nurse her. You been so good to us already and I don't like to ask again, miss, but . . ."

"Oh, Heddie, of course I'll go. I can leave right now. But can't you stay with her? We can go together. You should be with her now."

Heddie's face drooped with misery. "I can't, miss. I'd lose my job. Your aunt told me so. You know she means it. You go be with Mama and I won't worry. I'll be home early tonight." Heddie tried to smile, but her face fell again and tears ran down her cheeks. Daphne's heart wrenched. Why should Heddie work all day if her mother was dying? But she knew Aunt Elspeth wanted an excuse to fire the girl.

"I'll just put on my bonnet and leave a note to Papa and Aunt Elspeth telling them that I'll be out for the day." Daphne made her arrangements and then gathered together a few things to take to Heddie's house. She kissed Heddie good-bye and promised to send word if Mrs. Bronislavski's condition worsened.

The trip to Bayardstown seemed unusually long. Daphne knew that Heddie had had to leave her mother alone with her youngest brothers and sisters. The eldest three had all had to go to work to earn. The small children would be incapable of helping their mother if an emergency arose.

Crowds of people filled the streets, although it was not yet six o'clock. Housewives weaved their way to market, their tiny silver butter tasters hanging on twine around their necks, their keys swaying to and fro and clattering loudly. Market men pushed loads of fresh, dewy vegetables. Workers of every description, their faces pinched with the exhaustion of continual twelve-hour days, rushed to their jobs. The factories were spewing coal dust over the city, turning the bright blue sky a deep grey. Daphne was usually delighted by the crowds and the bustle of early morning in Pittsburgh, but this morning, everyone seemed bent on getting in her way and slowing her down. She felt as though she would never reach Bayardstown. The dream she had had that morning had filled her with foreboding.

When Daphne arrived at Mrs. Bronislavski's room, she was barely able to recognize the shrunken figure lying on the bed as Heddie's mother. The woman's sallow face rested weakly against the pillow, deep circles under her eyes. Her thin yellow hands picked weakly at the sheets, their flesh like paper. Daphne could barely contain her exclamation of horror. She never had seen a person so close to death. What made the scene all the more horrible was that Mrs. Bronislavski's body was swollen with her baby.

In later years, Daphne could remember little of those painful hours she spent with Mrs. Bronislavski and her small, bewildered children. Daphne was hopelessly unequipped to help Mrs. Bronislavski or to soothe the children who seemed almost as much afraid of her as they were of their mother's suffering. She chattered nervously for an hour, then lapsed into silence until Dr. Williams arrived.

Daphne took the children out of the room during the examination. They went willingly, having lost their fear of Daphne to their fear of the doctor. With his bristling mustache, he was an imposing figure, indeed. Baby Maria clung to Daphne's neck and buried her head against her shoulder as the small group stood in the dark hallway. The other children gathered around Daphne, the younger ones sucking their fingers. Suddenly Jan, who, at eight, was the eldest child not at work, said, "There's monsters and horrible things comes in this hall sometimes. But you'll protect us, huh?"

Daphne solemnly vowed that she would. Changing the subject, she asked if they wanted to hear a story.

"I know this story because it happened to me. When I was little, I used to be called Goldilocks."

Jan scoffed, "Nah, you wasn't. Your hair's red."

The happy interlude was broken by the arrival of Dr. Williams in the hallway. He told the children to go inside so that he could talk to Daphne alone. They left, a little reluctantly.

"She's a very sick woman. Her time is almost near and she's not strong enough to live through the delivery," said the doctor in brusque tones.

"What can I do to help? Can't you do anything?"

"I've done all I can. She's in God's hands now. Just keep her comfortable and call me when she begins labor. I think you should call the priest then, too, so he can give her last rites. I don't mean to be harsh, Miss Slater, but if you're going to nurse her, you have to know how matters stand. She hasn't long to live. She's a religious woman. In fact, I really think a priest should be sent for right away."

With that, the doctor turned on his heel and disappeared down the dingy stairs. Daphne bit her lip to keep from crying and tried to compose herself so that the children would not be frightened further. She then went back inside.

"Jan, did you go to church yesterday?"

"Yes. Heddie took us because Mama was too sick to go."

"Can you find your way there alone?"

He nodded.

"I want you to go over to the church and get the priest. Tell him your mama is sick and she'd like to hear Mass at home today."

A smile flickered across Mrs. Bronislavski's face. Her expression seemed to clear then and become calm. Jan put on his frayed cap and squared his shoulders, full of the importance of his mission.

"Take this with you, Jan." Daphne handed him a brief note that explained Mrs. Bronislavski's condition to the priest. "Be careful and come right back."

The children clustered around Daphne and demanded that she tell them the Goldilocks story. She was glad to. There was nothing she could do for Mrs. Bronislavski now. The woman was indeed in God's hands.

When Jan and the priest entered, a deep silence descended. Even tiny Maria was quiet and serious, sitting in Daphne's lap, her curly blonde head leaning against Daphne's shoulder. The priest was a thin, elderly man with a stern face, but kind eyes. He walked directly up to the sick woman and took her hands in his, speaking to her softly in Polish. For the first time that morning, Mrs. Bronislavski spoke. Her voice was inaudible except to the priest. The priest walked across the room to the kitchen table and opened his bag. Then he returned to Mrs. Bronislavski's bedside and began to say the Latin prayers. Mrs. Bronislavski's face shone with joy as she listened. Finally, the priest placed the host on Mrs. Bronislavski's tongue and she closed her eyes in blissful prayer. The priest spoke the last words, then sat down to say a silent prayer for the soul of the sick woman.

Daphne's own soul was touched by what she had witnessed. She had a new feeling of hope, which seemed peculiar since Mrs. Bronislavski's life in this world was nearly at an end.

The priest spoke to Mrs. Bronislavski again before he left, and then came over and blessed each of the children. Then he spoke to Daphne. "Maria asked me to thank you for all you have done for her and her family. Peace be with you, my child. You have done much good."

Daphne's eyes filled with tears as she watched the old priest close his case and leave the room. For a few moments there was silence. What had just passed was too important for speech. Even the youngest of the children sensed it.

The rest of the day was filled with the small tasks that provided the family with what comfort they could find. Daphne told stories to the children, fed them and cuddled them. She wiped Maria's brow and smoothed her pillow when she became restless. But even as she performed these small tasks, her mind was elsewhere. She was constantly thinking of Rene and how she could arrange to meet him and what she could say to warn him. He was a proud man and she had humiliated him by saying that she was engaged to Caleb Winters. Daphne could almost see his dark eyes turn to smoldering stone at the sight of her. Daphne sighed at the thought.

"You're tired, ain't you, Daphne?" asked Casimir, his small hand patting his cheek. "Mama used to sigh like that, but now she's too tired. Heddie says she's gonna take a long sleep and be with God. Heddie says she'll like that, but I think she'll miss us."

Daphne's eyes welled up with tears as she thought of Heddie's bravery in trying to prepare her younger brothers and sisters for something that she could not bear herself.

"Yes, Mama will like that. Heddie's right. You know, Casimir, when you're sleeping you don't miss people because you can dream of them, and then it seems as though they are there with you. That's nice, isn't it?"

"I guess. But what about bad dreams?" asked Casimir suspiciously.

"Mama's too good to have bad dreams, silly," answered Jan.

Daphne fed the children their lunch and tried to encourage Mrs. Bronislavski to eat some of the chicken broth she had brought with her, but the sickly woman could not eat. Daphne began to worry that she would be unable to go to the settlement house to teach her class at four. She did not like to leave the children alone, but she hated to miss the class.

"It's time for you to go teach your class at Miss Drummond's, ain't it, Daphne?" asked little Jan. "Heddie told me to walk you there. I'm the man of the family when Stan and Stefan are out at work."

"I don't think I should leave your mother alone," replied Daphne hesitantly.

"She ain't gonna be alone. Mrs. Amanti from downstairs is gonna be home by then. She's good friends with Mama."

Daphne decided that Mrs. Amanti could do anything she herself could, and so Jan pulled his cap on and kissed his mother good-bye, leaving Casimir in charge of the other children. "You watch them kids and don't let 'em wake Mama," he admonished as he escorted Daphne from the apartment.

Jan took Daphne by the hand and fairly pulled her down the street. "I like going to Miss Drummond's. Let's hurry," he cried.

Daphne's thoughts were already on the big old house. She hoped to see Rene there.

"Here we are. Here we are!" shrieked Jan. "Would it be all right if I came in? Just for a minute?"

"Of course, Jan. But then you have to go home to mind the other children. Maybe you could borrow a story book from the library."

Jan ran off without another word and Daphne went to teach her class. The hour-long class seemed interminable. The children were just as charming and eager to learn, but their teacher was preoccupied and worried. Daphne had to force herself not to constantly look out the door in hopes of seeing Rene walk by.

Finally, the last of the lessons was recited and the last of the children had filed out of the room and Daphne was alone. She went cold with fear when she thought of what might happen to Rene if she could not warn him in time. It was essential that she speak with him that day. Caleb could try to have Rene jailed at any time. She could wait no longer.

126

Determined, she sat down at her desk and picked up her pen.

Meet me where we first met at the same hour. Your life depends on it. D.

Daphne folded the paper and wrote Rene's name in a firm hand. She felt sure that Rene would understand the note and meet her at the quarry that night at midnight. Daphne walked softly to the residents' mailboxes and slipped in Rene's note with a silent prayer that it reach only him and not fall into the hands of Caleb's spy.

Daphne hurried to the Bronislavskis' to check on Heddie's mother before she went home. She went up to the weary invalid's bed and smoothed the wrinkled sheets. The doctor had advised her to give Mrs. Bronislavski some brandy occasionally and Daphne did so, glad she had thought to bring a bottle from home. The draft seemed to have a good effect on the woman, for soon afterward, with Daphne's help, she was able to swallow a little chicken broth.

Stan and Stefan arrived home from their day's labor in the coal mines just outside the city. Their small faces were smudged with coal dust, their eyes rimmed with it. They smiled at their mother. Each smile held a deep weariness. The boys worked as breakers, sorting the different sizes of coal as it came up to the surface. The work was backbreaking, done from a stooped position, and many of the boys who did it had permanently crooked backs as a result.

Before they could eat, the boys had to wash themselves. Their vigorous splashing in the wash basin seemed to bring out the boy in each of them, to temporarily banish the old men they had become. The water was soon black with coal. With the dust washed away, Daphne could see what the cruel work had done to the boys' hands. Each small hand was bloody, the fingertips crushed. The hard coal falling down the shoots had toppled on their hands, maiming their fingers.

Daphne cried out, "Your poor hands!"

"It's nothin', miss. All us boys got hands like this," shrugged Stefan. "How's Mama been?"

"Weak and tired, although she seems a bit better now."

Stan and Stefan walked up to their mother's bed and took her frail hands. The three spoke softly in Polish for a few minutes, the love between them apparent in every face.

"Mama says the priest come to give her last rites," said Stan.

"I think it comforted your mother a great deal," replied Daphne. "I brought some stew today. Would you like to eat now?"

Daphne and the children sat down to their dinner. Stan and Stefan ate ravenously, for they had had nothing since morning but bread and drippings and cold tea. After the dishes were washed, Daphne sat down and began to do some of the family's mending. Jan's knickers were in an especially sorry state. It appeared that he spent most of his time on his knees. The tiny room was crowded. Stan and Stefan sat at the table, Stan reading the paper and Stefan, his head on his arms, already asleep. The younger children crawled about the sloping wooden floor playing marbles.

Mrs. Bronislavski's moans brought a sudden end

to the tranquillity. They all rushed to her bedside. After a whispered conference between Stefan and his mother, Stefan informed Daphne that his mother's time had come and that she wanted him to fetch Mrs. Amanti.

After a few dreadful minutes during which Mrs. Bronislavski moaned loudly, Stefan returned with the capable Mrs. Amanti.

"Ah, *la povera* Maria," cried Mrs. Amanti, her face all sympathy. "Get them kids outta here. They can stay in my room. Is no good for them see their mama like this." The children filed out of the room reluctantly.

"Stefan!" called Daphne, "run and get Dr. Williams."

Mrs. Amanti bustled around the room, putting pots of water on the stove to boil and hanging towels on the racks above the stove to heat. In between she spoke reassuringly to Mrs. Bronislavski, who seemed to understand her despite the fact that the words of reassurance were spoken in a mixture of Italian and English. The Polish woman writhed in pain. Daphne stood in the middle of the room wondering what to do.

"Get more water," ordered Mrs. Amanti, thrusting a wooden bucket into Daphne's white, trembling hands. It was not that Mrs. Amanti needed more water, but rather that she needed an excuse to get Daphne out of the room. She feared that the girl would faint, for her cheeks had become pale and her lips tinged with blue.

Daphne fairly flew from the room, barely aware of the twists and turns in the dark stairs. Once outside in the courtyard, she gasped for air. How stifling the air in the small room above had been! She pulled at the pump handle with all her might, trying to push aside horrors crowding her mind. For Daphne, the horrors of what was going on upstairs were doubled because so much was unknown. She never had been told anything about how babies were born. It was not a suitable subject for young women still unmarried.

Daphne toiled up the stairs with the heavy water bucket, trying not to spill its contents. As she reached the last flight of steps, she braced herself. Just then she heard light, rapid footsteps running up the stairs behind her. Heddie's worried face appeared, her eyes large.

"Mama?" she asked, frantic that her mother had died while she had been away.

"Go to her," answered Daphne, and the girl flew past. As Daphne lifted the heavy bucket once more, there was a shriek. She froze. After what seemed an eternity, she forced herself to pick up the bucket again and continue upstairs.

When Daphne entered the room, she saw Heddie kneeling beside the bed, sobbing. Mrs. Bronislavski's form was still, and the baby lay beside her. It was dead. Daphne put down the bucket and, kneeling beside Heddie, put her arms around her.

"She was still alive when I came in," sobbed the distraught girl. "She told me not to cry after she was dead because she was going to join Papa." Here Heddie broke down once again.

There was a knock on the door and Stefan and the doctor came in. Stefan ran to his mother, took her lifeless hand and pressed it to his lips. Then he turned to his sister and the two sobbed in one another's arms. Mrs. Amanti sent Daphne to keep the children downstairs so that she could prepare their mother for burial.

When the children returned to the room half an hour later, their mother lay on the bed, her hair neat and tidy, her eyes closed, a peaceful expression on her face. They knelt around the bed to pray. Even baby Maria stood quietly, her tiny palms pressed. As Daphne looked at the devout family, tears came to her eyes.

When they had finished their prayers, they rose and Heddie spoke. "Thank you for all you did. You been good to us. We'll bury Mama tomorrow morning, I think, as we've no proper place to lay her out. Please come."

Daphne pressed Heddie's hand and nodded, too moved to speak. The children then thanked Mrs. Amanti. The woman hugged each of them to her ample breast and allowed her tears to mingle freely with theirs.

"Your mama was a good woman and now she in heaven," said Mrs. Amanti, making the sign of the Cross.

There was another knock at the door and Heddie went to answer it. Lilleth Drummond stepped into the room, her eyes searching to discover where she could be most helpful. Daphne looked at her with admiration, noting the sympathetic yet determined set of her mouth and the keen glance of her warm brown eyes.

"I'm so sorry. This is a sad night. Can I tell Father Marion to come in the morning?"

It was agreed that Lilleth would speak to the priest about the funeral.

"Will you sit up with her tonight?"

"Yes," answered Heddie, her lip trembling.

"Then I shall stay with you. I'll just go out to speak to the priest and then I'll come right back."

"Miss Daphne," said Heddie, "your aunt wants you at home. She's been looking for you all day."

Stan was sent to accompany Daphne home, despite her protests that she could get home alone. Both Heddie and Lilleth assured her that it would be unsafe for her to return home by herself, for it was past nine o'clock.

All the windows of the stately red brick mansion were lit. Daphne could discern her aunt and her father sitting in the front parlor, for the heavy satin drapes were not closed. She supposed that they would be angry with her for being so late and missing supper, and she steeled herself for the coming battle.

Hawkins had barely opened the front door to admit her when Aunt Elspeth appeared, her mouth set in its sternest line. "Your father would like to speak with you," she said, a threatening note in her voice.

"Very well, Aunt," replied Daphne, calmly taking off her shawl and bonnet and handing them to Hawkins along with her empty basket. She had taken on the responsibilities of a grown woman today and she would not be cowed.

The parlor looked especially formal tonight. The red damask wing chairs sat on either side of the marble fireplace. The horsehair sofa reigned in stiff dignity before the crackling fire. The silver coffee urn sat on its ornate silver tray, reflecting the firelight. But there was something missing. Daphne could no longer respect her father, not with all she knew. She still loved him, but after what she had overheard, she could only pity him. The entire house and its fittings, the very clothes on their backs, rested on a lie, the lie of her father's prosperity. Looking at Jeb Slater, Daphne saw a ruined and shrunken man, a man who could be bought.

"What is the meaning of this?" blustered Jeb.

"Papa?"

"Don't play the simpleton, Daphne. Where have you been all day? Your aunt has been worried sick."

"She shouldn't have been. I left a note when I went out this morning. I was nursing a sick woman and couldn't come home because she took a turn for the worse. She's dead now."

"Charity is all well and good, but your first duty is to your family. Nursing is not fit for a girl your age. Elspeth certainly can find something charitable for you to do at home. Knitting, or something similar."

"I think that I'm old enough to find my own occupations. Knitting does little good. There are people in real need, right here in Pittsburgh."

"I'll not have you preaching at me, young lady. You're still young enough to be sent to your room. You may go there until you can speak civilly to me."

"I'll go, but only because I'm tired. And I was speaking civilly to you, Papa. Good night."

Daphne left the room after a final glance at her father, his face red, his small mouth pouting. The clock in the hallway struck ten. Daphne sighed. It was two hours until she could see Rene to warn him. He had to come to the quarry! He had to read her note!

Daphne undressed, turned out the light and lay in bed feigning sleep until she heard the big clock strike eleven-thirty.

She managed to dress and slip out of the house

without encountering anyone, and she breathed more freely when she was far away from the house. Daphne blended in well with the dark June night, for she wore a black dress and had wrapped a black shawl around her head and shoulders. She looked like a serving woman returning home late from one of the mansions on Lower Penn Street.

The woods closed around Daphne like a welcoming blanket and she walked rapidly. She prayed with all her soul that Rene would be at the quarry. As she reached the clearing a hand shot out, catching her arm and pulling her into the bushes. Daphne gasped, but managed not to cry out. A familiar voice hissed, "Quiet!" into her ear. Just then a group of men passed, not two feet away from where she had been on the path.

When they were well away her captor whispered, "Why did you ask me here?" in a voice filled with emotion.

For a few moments she could not speak. Rene was too close. His arm still held her.

"You had no romantic purpose in mind, I trust. I don't fancy meeting engaged women even if I hate their fiancés."

Daphne was stung and she pulled away from Rene. "I came to warn you that your life is in danger."

"Is that all?"

"Listen to me! I overheard Caleb Winters telling my father that he has placed a spy in your group. This man will give evidence against you. False, but the courts will believe it."

After a shocked silence, Rene asked, "Do you know who it is?"

"No names were mentioned. I'll try to find out. Please, you must be careful. You could be hanged. Caleb wants you dead," cried Daphne, her hand finding Rene's and gripping it tightly.

Rene laughed. "I knew he was plotting against me. And I had suspected there was a spy. Thank you for warning me, Daphne. But tell me, isn't it rather strange for a woman to be an informant against her own fiancé? After all, he is the man you love," added Rene.

"I don't love Caleb," replied Daphne hotly. Before Rene could reply, she pulled away. "I must leave now. I have told you this because I fear for your life. I'll try to find out the spy's name. Be careful." And with that, Daphne turned and ran down the path.

Chapter 11

The black hearse, drawn by a sturdy dray horse, moved slowly through the streets of Bayardstown to the cemetery at the edge of the city. Passers-by looked sympathetically at the small, ragged party following the hearse on foot. The eight children wept silently, holding one another's hands for comfort.

Some onlookers might have wondered at the two well-dressed women who accompanied the little band of children. Those who lived in the neighborhood knew the chestnut head and stark black dress of Lilleth Drummond. She often accompanied a grieving family to the last resting place of a loved one. But who was the young beauty?

In fifteen minutes' walk, they reached a wooded part of the city. Maple trees in full leaf shaded the narrow lane. The children's pale faces seemed even paler in the sunshine. The coffin was unloaded from the hearse by the driver and the two older boys. Father Marion opened his worn prayer book and spoke.

"My children, you must not grieve too much for your mother, for she has, by the grace of the Virgin Mary, gone to Heaven to join our Lord, Jesus Christ. She is happy and at peace there, in company with your father and relieved of the sorrows of this life. Think of her looking down on you and speak to her every day in your prayers."

Heddie sobbed. She had promised her mother that she would not cry and she knew that her mother was at peace now, yet she missed her so much. How would they manage without their mother to hold them together? Who would mind the younger children while she, Stan and Stefan went to work? Heddie cried from both grief and fear.

The coffin was lowered into the ground and the children filed up in turn and threw flowers onto the coffin.

"I think it's time we went home," said Lilleth, putting her arm around Heddie's shoulder. She did not want the children to see the dirt piled on top of their mother's coffin. "I was thinking that it might be a good idea if Mary Ann, Cecelia and Maria spent their days at the nursery school."

Heddie cast her a grateful look and thanked her. The little group then dispersed and Daphne left for home. Aunt Elspeth was waiting for her in the parlor and Daphne thought, Can she have seen me go out last night? I don't think so. I can just see by her expression that she wants to give me a good talking to. Daphne wearily hung up her shawl and bonnet and went into the parlor.

She sat down, making sure that her back was perfectly straight and her hands clasped in her lap.

Her aunt sat on the couch, her wide skirts spreading stiffly about her.

"You have been disobedient, I fear."

"What do you mean, Aunt?" asked Daphne, feigning innocence.

"It's a sad matter when a child is so often disobedient that she cannot recall which of her many wrongs she is being taken to task for. But leaving that aside, I will tell you that I refer to those Bayardstown people. Your father told you last night that you were to have nothing more to do with them. Yet, that is where you were this morning, were you not? What have you to say for yourself?"

"Those people are my friends. They can't help it if they're poor."

"You are a child, Daphne, so I'll overlook your foolishness and attempt to educate you. Such people can't be your friends. You and they have nothing in common and that is that. You may be able to help them through appropriate charitable agencies, but you yourself may have nothing to do with them.

"Such people are poor due to prodigality, idleness and drink. Their wages are sufficient, but they are undisciplined and slovenly. Providing those people with money or help merely encourages them in their vicious ways. I should hope you'll be guided by my advice. No man will want you for a wife if you continue to associate with such people. You are known by the company you keep, my dear."

Elspeth closed her lips in a line of smug satisfaction. She had done her duty and was pleased with herself. If Daphne wished to follow a course of ruin and dishonor, it would not be on Elspeth's head.

There obviously was no point in arguing, so

Daphne bade her aunt good-bye and went upstairs. She listened carefully for the sounds of her aunt's departure from the house to attend a Ladies Christian Missionary Society meeting.

Daphne then crept stealthily downstairs and entered her father's study, shutting the door softly behind herself. She listened carefully to be sure that she had not been detected. The house was completely quiet. Her father was at his office downtown and Aunt Elspeth had just left. Daphne breathed a sigh of relief: she would have at least half an hour to look through her father's papers for the name of the spy in Rene's group.

Jeb Slater's study was a small room at the back of the house. It overlooked the river and allowed him to watch his barges chugging down the river, bringing iron from the vast fields near Lake Superior. His roll-top desk took up most of the space in the room. The desk was open, its surface littered with papers. Jeb's chair was pushed back from the desk. The room gave the impression that he had just left it and would return at any moment.

Though not sure what she was looking for, Daphne began to sift through her father's papers, looking for anything relating to Rene or the Knights of Labor. Daphne's search for the spy's name proved fruitless. She doubted that her father even knew it. There was probably only one man who knew who the spy was: the man who had employed him to entrap Rene, and that man was Caleb Winters.

"I'll have to figure out a way to go through Caleb's desk as well. Perhaps I should call upon Catherine and try to get a few minutes alone in

Caleb's study," she said softly to herself, biting her lower lip in nervousness.

With a determined step, Daphne went upstairs to dress for her call on Catherine. Although Daphne had learned nothing about Rene's problems from snooping in her father's desk, she had learned a great deal about her father's own business troubles.

The amount of money he's spent is just immense, she thought as she pulled on a gown. It's no wonder he has none left. Why, he must own nearly every iron mine around Lake Superior. Or at least Superior Mines does and as near as I can tell, he and Superior Mines are one and the same thing. It's a shame that just when he had control of the iron market, the price fell so low. Why, if the price were still high, we'd be rich again!

Daphne had stumbled upon the papers relating to Jeb Slater's dealings with the mine owners of the Lake Superior region. She had found letters from the mine owners begging her father to reduce the rates he charged on his barges for taking their iron to the markets of Pittsburgh and Philadelphia. Letters of a later date, addressed to Superior Mines, offered these same mines for sale at low prices; they had been forced out of business by the ruinous transport costs Jeb had levied on them. And still later came letters from the new managers of these mines, now owned by Superior Mines, bemoaning the fallen price of iron and the difficulties of making a profit. Last of all came letters from a number of banks asking for more prompt payment of the loans that had made possible the purchase of the mines.

Daphne understood enough of business to know that her father had been playing a dangerous game, one with all-or-nothing stakes. By gaining control of the iron mines, he controlled all of the most important cargo for his barges. But more important, he could control the price of the precious ore. He could refuse to sell if the price dropped too low. Yet, he had not been able to earn enough from the sale of the ore to repay his bank loans. The current depression was too severe and Jeb had quite simply been too optimistic and taken out too many loans. Daphne now understood why he so badly needed Caleb's help and why Caleb was so willing to give it to him. The mines would one day be worth a fortune to the man who could retain ownership now!

"Daphne! This is the second time I've asked you. How shall I do your hair?" Letty interrupted Daphne's reverie.

"Oh, I don't know. Do what you like," answered Daphne abstractedly, her mind preoccupied with what she had learned that morning.

Letty ignored Daphne's mood and carefully arranged her glowing tresses. Then she selected an olive-colored lacework snood to match Daphne's afternoon dress of black and olive striped silk and pinned it along the crown of Daphne's head.

"There you are, my girl. Come out of your sulks and look at yourself," announced Letty, smoothing Daphne's dress.

"I'm not sulking, I'm just thinking. You've done a fine job, Letty," answered Daphne, looking critically at herself in the mirror. The dress was extremely becoming if a trifle old for her. The gleaming of the silk softened the somber colors of the fabric. The overskirt was looped in back to reveal an underskirt.

"Will you tell Hawkins to have the carriage

brought around? I'll be going out directly. Oh, and get my parasol as well, please.'"

"Good afternoon, James. Is Miss Catherine at home?"

"She isn't receiving callers this afternoon, Miss Slater, but I'm sure she'll be pleased to see you. I'll tell her you are here."

"Very good. I'll wait for her in Mr. Caleb's study," answered Daphne, fearful that James would forbid her to enter that sanctuary.

"As you will, Miss Slater," was the answer she received. He was too good a servant to question the wishes of his employers' guests, yet he did take note of unusual behavior.

Daphne walked nervously down the short corridor that led to Caleb's study. The Winters' house, although grandly named Winterhaven, was barely more than a large clapboard cottage set on a quiet side street. One entered the yard through a vine-covered latticed arch, which in June was fragrant with wisteria. The house was quite comfortable for two. Caleb frequently was heard to say that he would not move to a grander house until he had a wife to run it. All the rooms were small, but pleasantly furnished in the style of the 1850s. Current fashion dictated heavier furniture. Caleb's study contained a simple deal table and straight-backed chair, an old but fine Oriental carpet, and a well-stocked bookcase. Daphne's heart sank when she saw how neat the desk was. On top of the desk were a blotter, an inkstand and a small diary.

Perhaps he has made some note of the man in his diary, thought Daphne, glancing hopefully at the small morocco-bound book. She picked it up and leafed through its pages, looking for possible clues. It was a diary of Caleb's social engagements, and while she found many references to herself, she found nothing that seemed relevant to the labor movement.

As she touched the desk drawer, attempting to open it, she heard a noise and turned toward the door.

"Oh, Catherine. You startled me," said Daphne.

"I should say so. But what are you doing in here? An odd place to wait, if I may say so."

"Well, um, if I'm to marry your brother, I ought to try to learn all I can about him. I wanted to see where he spends so much of his time."

Catherine threw her arms around Daphne's neck and kissed her. "Oh, I'm so pleased. At last we'll really be sisters! When did you decide? Oh, tell me all about it!" cried Catherine, her pale cheeks flushed with excitement.

"No! I didn't mean I was going to marry him. I haven't decided. I mean, I probably won't. I . . . don't want to."

"Oh, Daphne, I wish you wouldn't get me all excited like that for no reason. Do be more careful. Shall we go into my sitting room? It's so dull and dark down here. That is, if you've finished satisfying your curiosity about Caleb. I'll have to tell on you."

"Oh, don't," cried Daphne more vehemently than she had intended. Noting Catherine's puzzled expression, Daphne amended, "You know how Caleb carries on and snaps at you. I just don't want him getting annoyed at you on account of me. He might not like it that I was in here. It was silly of me," finished Daphne lamely.

The two girls left the room arm in arm and walked to Catherine's sitting room on the southwest side of the house. It was a pleasant room looking out on the rose garden at the back of the house. Today with all the windows open and the roses in full bloom, it smelled wonderful. Like the rest of the house, it was furnished simply. Catherine's collection of Venetian glass in a rainbow of hues stood on a shelf built into one of the windows, spilling brilliant colors across the pale pink Oriental rug. Drawings and water colors that Catherine had done hung on the walls and a crewel fire screen she was making stood before her work desk. Next to the table was the small spinet Catherine played so beautifully.

"Whenever I come in here I am reminded of what an accomplished person you are, Catherine. It puts me to shame. I wish I could do half the things you can. Drawing and playing the spinet and needlework. I'm so clumsy at all that," sighed Daphne.

"You could do all the things I do if you wanted to, and better, because you are more clever than I. But these things don't interest you much," replied Catherine. "But I haven't told you my news."

"What is it?"

"Caleb thinks I should marry."

"Really?" Daphne lifted an eyebrow. "And whom does he think you should marry?"

"Tad Billinghurst," blushed Catherine, turning away in embarrassment.

"So! Are you happy?" asked Daphne, astounded at Catherine's news. Not two weeks before, Tad had been pledging his undying love to *her*. She had expected him to get over it, but not quite this quickly!

147

"Of course. It is what Caleb wants and Mrs. Billinghurst is so very pleased. Tad is quite pleasant."

"It sounds to me as though you don't care a fig for Tad. Do you love him?"

"Love comes after marriage, Daphne. I'm sure we'll grow to love one another."

"Well, I'm not," replied Daphne sternly.

"I had so hoped that you'd be pleased with my news. We can't all be like you, withstanding everything and everyone to do as we want. I'm not like that. I do as I am bidden. It's my nature."

"How can you ever be happy letting yourself be ruled by others?"

"I couldn't be happy forcing my own way and making those I love unhappy. I think Tad and I will come to suit one another admirably. We have much in common and were childhood friends. I'm content, Daphne. Please don't badger me to act as you act. We can love one another, but we never can be the same. To act as you do would kill me. I am a frailer flower than you. The hothouse rose can't live where its wild cousin thrives. That is how we are. Let it be. Now, shall we have tea?" finished Catherine.

The two girls dropped the issue and enjoyed a pleasant visit.

Chapter 12

The day began in oppressive heat with dawn breaking through a clouded sky. Clouds of smoke hovered over the valley, cutting off all fresh air. The atmosphere was thick with moisture and black with coal dust.

Daphne sat on the brocaded couch in her sitting room, fanning herself beneath the flickering gaslights. Although it was only ten o'clock in the morning, the gas was on, for the clouds of smoke and dust made everything seem almost as dark as night.

If only it would rain, thought Daphne, then it would not be so terribly hot and dark. I can't bear this suffocating atmosphere for another moment! She leapt up from her indolent pose and paced the room with remarkable energy.

I feel as though I ought to be doing something, she mused. Heddie is troubled. Rene is in danger. Yet, here I am doing nothing. I feel so useless.

She continued to pace the small, well-decorated

151

sitting room, a creature at odds with her surroundings. The china figurines on the mantelpiece seemed to mock Daphne's tempestuous feelings by their cool surfaces and set smiles. Daphne stopped before the collection of shepherdesses and great ladies and stared at them intently.

"You sit and do nothing all day, content with your lot, happy to be dressed prettily and powdered nicely. Father buys me figurines when he is on business trips because he wishes I, too, were a china doll. But I can't be. I'm not like you. I must act and be and do. I can't sit forever in this parlor and let the world go on without me. Oh, if only I knew what to do!" she muttered. A light came into Daphne's eyes and she announced to the china figurines, "I'll go see Miss Drummond."

Daphne fled the room and collected her bonnet, shawl and reticule. Once more she was on her way to Bayardstown and away from the life her family had so carefully charted for her. Her spirits soared.

The intensity of the heat kept people off the streets. The streets of Bayardstown, usually teeming, were nearly empty. Even shopkeepers had drawn their shutters and taken their goods inside. The air seemed heavier than it had earlier and the blackness of coal clouds was now tinged with the bruised dark blue of thunderheads.

Daphne glanced at the sky and quickened her pace, hurrying toward the settlement house. The poverty of the town was more noticeable with the streets empty. Buildings were in disrepair. Bits of trash blew about on the dusty streets. Coal dust blew into Daphne's eye and she drew her shawl more closely around her head and face.

The wind picked up and battled with her long skirts, alternately blowing them about or flattening them against her frame. Daphne struggled to hold her skirts down as she tried to hold her shawl in place. Suddenly Daphne felt very tired and longed to rest. She feared that she never would reach the settlement house and the reassuring smile of Lilleth Drummond.

A shutter flapped against one of the houses, causing Daphne to start. She looked around in an effort to discover where the sound had come from. She saw the loose shutter and heard it bang again, but then she also saw a group of men standing in front of a saloon, watching her. She could not make out their faces. She faced forward again, heading into the wind, and quickened her pace. Daphne had no real reason to fear them, but she felt afraid. Why were they watching her?

She resisted the impulse to turn around to see if they were following her and stumbled forward into the stormy afternoon, her skirts whipping against her legs. Daphne silently cursed fashion for making her wear such impractical clothes. A fierce gust of wind blew up, flinging her bonnet off her head and untying its strings as though by magic. She tried in vain to catch it as it was carried away by the wind. As she turned to see where the bonnet had gone, she saw that the men from the saloon were following her, handkerchiefs held to their faces.

Daphne began to run, holding up her long skirts with both hands. Her shawl fell away, a brightly colored bit of flowered calico contrasting with the street dust. An alley beckoned her. She thought that perhaps she could hide in it or lose her pursuers in a maze of side streets. She struggled to breathe deeply, her heart pounding in fear. She thought she heard footsteps behind her coming closer and closer.

Daphne turned to face her attackers, unable to run any longer. She stood, wild-eyed; her long hair blowing wildly. The crowd of men closed in, yelling.

"What have I done?" Daphne cried out.

"Spy!" One of the masked men hissed the answer. The wind howled fiercely and the first drops of rain hit them.

One of the men grabbed Daphne roughly by the arm. She struggled against him, kicking at his legs and screaming. At that moment someone came up swiftly behind her and hit her over the head. She sank to the ground, unconscious.

Daphne awoke abruptly and immediately began to struggle against the arms that held her. The rain continued to fall in heavy drops, hitting her face and neck and mingling with her tears. She was sobbing with fear and pain. The back of her head felt wet and warm, throbbing from the blow.

"Let me go! Let me go!" she cried, struggling to get up. The only sounds she could hear were the pounding in her ears and the noise of the storm that engulfed her. The night was dark and her attacker's face was almost invisible.

"Daphne, Daphne!" She knew that voice. "Don't struggle so, my darling. Don't you know me? Oh, what have they done to you?" He held her tightly.

It was Rene! Rene must have betrayed her. He was trying to kill her.

"Let me go! Why do you want to kill me?"

"Kill you? Beloved Daphne, what are you saying? You are still faint from loss of blood and those hoodlums could be just around the corner. Do you think you can stand? We must get away from here. If they come back, they may bring more men and I may not be able to fight them off this time."

"You mean you weren't trying to kill me?" Daphne asked weakly.

"Of course not. Daphne, I never could hurt you."

Rene picked her up, looking down tenderly at her face, stained with blood and dirt. He hurried toward the settlement house, bearing Daphne as though she were the most precious thing in the world.

Daphne relaxed in his strong arms, enjoying the feel of his warm chest against her cheek.

"Rene," she whispered, "I know it's not proper of me to ask, but do you love me?"

"Yes," was the prompt reply.

"I'm not really engaged to Caleb, you know," she confessed. "I just said that to make you angry."

"Hush. We'll talk about all of this later. For now, just keep still until I can get you inside. You should be looked at by a doctor."

Daphne shut her eyes and leaned against Rene, her heart singing. He loved her! The throbbing at the back of her head no longer mattered.

The next two hours passed in a blur as Lilleth Drummond tucked Daphne into bed in one of the rooms in the big old house and sent for the doctor. Rene settled into the oak chair beside her.

"I really feel perfectly well. When you found me in the street, I was just a little dazed and frightened," protested Daphne.

"When I found you, you were lying unconscious, and being set upon by a group of thugs. You aren't moving from this bed until the doctor gets here. You have a serious head wound. Oh, why couldn't I have been just a few minutes earlier?" Rene sighed. "Daphne, I warned you that the man who wrote you that note meant business."

Rene sighed again and held his head in his hands, his knuckles showing white against his swarthy skin. Daphne was sorry to see him so upset, but elated to know how deeply he cared for her.

He lifted his head and gazed at her. "Did you recognize any of them?"

"No, it was dark and they all wore handkerchiefs over their faces. But why did they call me a spy? I don't understand."

"They must think you're coming here to spy on them for your father. They may have heard that you were found hiding near one of our meetings. I hate to say it but one of the men in my own group is probably involved."

Daphne smiled at him and said softly, "I would almost thank them for bringing us together after all of our misunderstandings. Oh, Rene, I love you so much."

Rene stroked Daphne's forehead very gently and looked down at her, love shining from his grey eyes. He thought he had never seen a more beautiful face than Daphne's. And the eyes that returned his passionate gaze held an equally passionate intensity.

"Let's never let anything separate us again, Rene."

"Be still now and shut your eyes. I've been wrong and selfish to let you talk. Try to sleep, Daphne."

She drifted off, to be awakened a few minutes later by the doctor's arrival. When he had finished his examination and bandaged her head, swathing it in white gauze, the doctor said, "You are a very lucky young woman. You might have been hurt very badly. As it is, you'll probably ache a bit and feel weak for several days, but there is no serious harm done. A strong girl like you will be well soon." He patted her hand. "I'll tell Miss Drummond that it's safe to move you. Someone must accompany you home, however. Your family will be worried about you."

Daphne quaked at the idea of facing her father and aunt. They would be furious when they saw what had resulted from her disobedience.

"I hate to leave you and go home," she told Rene as soon as the doctor had left.

"It won't be for long. We'll be together soon. Don't look so sad. When you're all better, we'll meet at the quarry at midnight."

"I'm well right now. We can meet tonight," she answered.

"That we will not. You heard what the doctor said. I'll meet you there in five days, no sooner."

"You're so cruel," answered Daphne with a smile. "Why won't you let me have my way?"

"Because it won't help your recovery. Now listen to your elders," he teased.

"You are an insufferable old man," she retorted, making a face. Then she said slowly, "I think that I'll tell Papa and Aunt that robbers attacked me. I don't want them to know anything about the threatening note or my going to the quarry at night."

"That's probably a good idea," Rene agreed.

Lilleth helped Daphne out of bed and Rene carried her downstairs into a waiting carriage. There was no way he could take her home without causing more trouble, so Lilleth Drummond was her escort.

Inside the carriage, Daphne was aware of the pain in her head for the first time since the attack. Each jolt of the carriage sent a shooting spark through her spine and lodged in her aching head.

"You're in pain, my dear," said Miss Drummond sympathetically. "I wish there was something I could do, but I fear that I've left the best medicine standing outside the settlement house staring after us. You love Rene very much, don't you?"

"Does it show?" Daphne flushed.

"Yes. It's a lovely thing to see two people happy together. I wish you much luck together and I'm afraid, my dear, that you will need it. Many people will not be as happy for you as I am. Rene is a workingman. He is honest and good and he's struggled hard against poverty, but that won't matter to some people. They'll think him beneath you. I wish you luck, Daphne, and I'll help you all I can. I know what it is to go against society's conventions."

Daphne was just about to ask what she meant when they arrived at the Slater mansion. Lilleth went in with her and smoothed matters over with Jeb and Elspeth. She saw Daphne safely to her room. For that night, at least, Daphne was free of Jeb and Elspeth's anger. She fell asleep joyful in the knowledge of Rene's love.

Chapter 13

It was a fine July evening. A bright full moon rose, its silvery light reflecting across the river and dappling the treetops. Daphne was delighted to be out of the house and on her way to meet Rene. The five days of being housebound had been dreadfully dull. Aunt Elspeth had sat at her bedside, reading aloud from the Bible, occasionally alternating that with the collected sermons of Henry Ward Beecher. Daphne had wanted to scream. Her father had looked in on her every evening, his face showing worry over her health and anger at her disobedience. Each minute Daphne was thinking of Rene, wondering where he was and what he was doing.

Finally the joyous day had arrived. Daphne looked forward to the cup of warm milk her aunt gave her each night as she had never looked forward to milk before, for that meant that in a few minutes her aunt would plump up the pillows, remind her to say her prayers, and retire for the night.

Once Daphne was sure that the entire household was asleep, she crept out of bed and dressed herself as though for her wedding. Everything had to be perfect. She wanted Rene to think her beautiful. She wore a simple white eyelet dress with a stand-up collar. The sleeves were long and the skirt plain, lacking any bustle and having only one long ruffle at the bottom. The fine, light material with its floral openwork pattern kept the dress from seeming too severe and the simplicity marked it as a young girl's dress. Daphne pulled the sash tightly around her narrow waist and tied it into a large bow at the back. She turned in front of her mirror, examining herself in the moonlight, and then sat down at her dressing table to put up her hair.

The moonlight made her seem very pale. It hid the roses in her cheeks and the red of her lips. Daphne smiled at the spectral image of herself and began to brush out her hair. Parting it in the middle, she drew forward the two front sections while she twisted the back around her head. The front sections were then twisted around to form a circle around the back. Daphne inserted ivory combs deftly into her hair and looked at herself in the mirror.

"Oh, I don't look like myself! I can't wear it that way!"

Daphne sighed, took out the combs, shook her hair loose and recombed it. Why could she never look like the ladies in fashion magazines? She settled on leaving her hair loose, pulled back from her face by the ivory combs. The clock struck eleven-thirty and Daphne, shoes in hand, eased open the door, listening carefully. She walked softly out of the house and into the fragrant garden where she sat on a bench in the shadow of a wisteria arbor and put on her white kid shoes, lacing them impatiently.

Finally Daphne found herself out on the road, her heart singing. She pulled her black cashmere cloak more carefully around her, checking to be sure that it covered her white dress and that its hood covered her hair. A step on the gravel behind her caused her to whirl.

"Rene!" she cried, running to him. "I thought you were waiting for me at the quarry."

"I was afraid to let you walk so far. How is your head?"

"Perfect. Everyone was silly to worry so. I was barely injured at all."

"We must hurry on. It isn't wise for us to be seen together. Keep your cloak wrapped tightly and walk ahead of me as though you don't know me. I'll be behind watching to see that no one is following you."

"Oh, no! I want to talk with you," she cried, but a look from Rene silenced her.

Daphne walked briskly along the side of the road, anxious to reach the safety of the woods where she and Rene could be together without fear. I love him so much and yet I hardly know him, she marveled to herself. I have so much to say to him. I want him to tell me everything about himself. Yet, strangely, there really is no need for that. I feel as though we have known one another always.

Although he was hardly a naive schoolboy, Rene was experiencing similar feelings. The woman walking ahead of him fascinated him. She was lovely, charming. His luck in finding Daphne amazed him. He sighed, wishing things were not so difficult. She doesn't know what she's getting into. If she loves me, it will change her life drastically. Maybe she's too young to make that choice. I should make it for her, and send her home. I should lie to her and tell her I don't love her.

But I can't, Rene admitted to himself. I love her too much to give her up. Oh, beloved Daphne, I can't give you up, though I probably should. Rene continued to do battle with himself until they arrived at the quarry.

A fallen log provided a bench for them and they sat, gazing at one another intently. For a long time they sat without moving, content merely to look, and to be together. Then they moved closer, touching each other's face, tracing their outlines with gentle fingertips. Daphne marveled at the softness of his cheeks, how downy they were on the high cheekbones where his beard did not grow. She followed the course of his straight, proud nose and then outlined the curves of his ears, which anyone except a lover would have considered a bit large. She smiled. He was perfection.

Rene could resist no longer. He took her in his arms and tenderly pressed his mouth to hers. A thrilling tingle ran along Daphne's spine.

They kissed for a long time. And then Daphne felt his lips moving down her slender neck to her breasts. Rene rested his head against her firm, rounded bosom and she sighed deeply. Tentatively, she caressed his neck, reaching her hand inside his shirt and lovingly stroking his strong chest.

Rene raised his head and looked questioningly into Daphne's eyes. Yes, her heart answered, yes. Then aloud she breathed it so quietly that it was almost just a breath, a whisper. They stood up slowly, still gazing at one another. He touched her face, then reached around to the back of her dress and unbuttoned it. She stood absolutely still while he did so, watching his expression go from tender to passionate. Soon they both were naked. Rene folded Daphne in his arms and they lay down together in the grass. Passion overwhelmed them and carried them away. They were exquisitely sensitive to one another and moved as one until they reached a final crescendo of emotion that left them both spent and fulfilled.

Daphne looked at Rene, her eyes glowing. She nestled her head against his shoulder, her whole body relaxed. Then she shivered slightly. She reached out and pulled her cloak over them.

"I love you, Daphne," whispered Rene, hugging her closer to him. "You are my wife."

"Yes," she murmured. It was all so very simple there alone in the woods. They belonged to one another. They had been joined together by what they had experienced that night and nothing could tear them apart.

They lay in one another's arms, talking far into the night, planning their future, making silly jokes, telling one another how deep their love was.

"We must leave this city," Rene decided. "We can't love each other here. Will you come away with me?"

"Oh, yes. Of course. You are everything to me, Rene. I do love Pittsburgh, but I agree we can't stay here. Everyone will be against us. Can we go tomorrow?"

"Ah, you're so impulsive and free! I love that about you. We can't very well go tomorrow, but we'll go soon."

They held one another closely in the fleeting last moments of the night and then drew apart, aching at the separation. Daphne's dress was wrinkled and stained with grass, but she did not notice.

They walked out to the road, lingering a bit along the path. In the shadow of the oak trees, they exchanged one last tender, lingering kiss, a seal to the promises they had made. It gave them hope to face the days ahead. Suddenly Rene became apprehensive. What if they were separated?

"Daphne," he whispered urgently, his grey eyes troubled, "let's meet at the train depot at four o'clock. You are right. We can't stay here another day."

She threw her arms around him in response.

The last of the stars still lingered in the sky as they walked hand in hand toward the Slater mansion. A silence held them until they reached the red brick house.

"Soon, my darling," promised Rene, as he kissed Daphne's upturned face.

"Four o'clock," she murmured.

Then he was gone.

Chapter 14

Daphne stretched luxuriously in her bed, throwing her bare arms over her head and smiling happily. *Everything is perfect this morning. My wedding day!* Daphne's body tingled with an exquisite sense of physical well-being. Her muscles surged with energy and she executed a few impromptu dance steps across her bedroom floor. Catching sight of herself in the mirror, she stopped and stared.

I do look different! So happy, she thought wonderingly. *At last Rene and I can be together for always.* She hugged herself with joy at the thought of Rene and the new life they would be embarking on together that day. It was almost too good to be true.

There was so much to do. She had to pack, but secretly, and gather all her jewels to have something to sell when funds were needed. Daphne pulled on a peach-colored silk robe and stepped into her slippers, then poked her head out of her door. Before she could call for Letty, she sensed something strange downstairs. Her father's voice reached her.

"What you've just told me, although it's been very painful, is worth a great deal and I thank you. Now go, please. I've paid you well enough."

"I don't call ten dollars good pay, even if it is in gold," grumbled a man's voice. "Not after what I've told you."

Daphne crept closer to the staircase to hear better and perhaps catch a glimpse of the stranger who was speaking. This must be something to do with Rene. This might be the spy!

"It's not every day a man gives you good information like this. Your daughter's about to run off with a miner and you should be grateful that I heard 'em planning it. It's me you have to thank for stopping them."

Daphne started, her heart leaping, but she didn't stay to hear more. She ran swiftly to her room, shutting the door carefully behind her.

I must leave before Papa comes up here. I'm sure that he'll try to stop me from going away with Rene, she realized. Daphne dressed in a feverish hurry, pulling garments from the closet helter-skelter and putting them on. She grabbed her reticule and stuffed the contents of her jewel box into it. There were several dollars in her piggy bank, but she was afraid to break it because of the noise. Ready at last, she walked silently down the backstairs to the kitchen, and out to the stables.

"Morning, Miss Daphne," greeted Parsons, appearing from behind the door.

"Good morning, Parsons. Please bring Coral out to me immediately."

170

Parsons stared at her in astonishment. Daphne Slater was a girl of odd whims, but he never had known her to go riding in anything but a perfectly tailored riding habit. He was no expert on female apparel, but choosing to ride in a gown struck him as decidedly odd.

"Stop gawking and bring me my horse," ordered Daphne sharply, trying to sound angry instead of nervous. The old man turned and hurried to Coral's stall.

Every moment seemed a century to Daphne. She expected to hear her father's voice at any moment. But Parsons had done his job quickly and brought Coral outside. The old man then returned to the stable to get Coral's saddle. Daphne put her reticule on a ledge high up on the barn wall and then, gathering her skirts in one hand, she leapt astride the horse. Grabbing the reticule, she kicked the horse sharply and they were on their way. She'd decided to go to the settlement house. She remembered that Miss Drummond had promised to help them.

Parsons came out of the stable in time to see Daphne disappearing down the lane in a cloud of dust. He shook his head in confusion.

As she rode, Daphne was able to think more clearly. She wondered where Rene was and decided to try to find him so that they could be married immediately and leave the city before another moment was lost. She knew her father would do anything he could to stop her from marrying Rene.

Daphne tried to think of where Rene was most likely to be. She did not think that he would be working at the mine today, although he might have gone there to pick up his pay. The settlement house definitely was the best place to go, for they would know where Rene was.

Daphne spurred Coral onward, talking to her reassuringly. The horse was a bit startled at being ridden astride and without a saddle.

Pittsburgh was greeted by a strange sight that morning. A young woman, her long reddish-blonde hair streaming out behind her, was riding bareback, astride a roan mare whose coat was much the same color as its rider's hair. Daphne felt suddenly uneasy. There were a great many people in the streets milling around silently, anxiously. Coral felt it too and became skittish. Daphne struggled to calm her as she urged the mare through the streets of Pittsburgh toward the safety of the settlement house.

The shutters of Simpson's Dry Goods Emporium were closed. A man with a gun stood in front of the store, looking cautiously about. Daphne noticed that Simpson's was not the only store with its shutters closed and a man posted outside. What was happening?

It was with great relief that Daphne approached the stately old settlement house. She tied Coral to the hitching post and ran up the steps to the porch. The door was locked!

Daphne was shocked. That door was always open during the day. It was a policy of the house. She rang the bell firmly and waited, but no one came. What was wrong? Daphne couldn't think what to do next. She had come to a dead end.

Hopelessly, she sat down on the porch, her sense of despair almost overwhelming. Tears began to well up in her eyes. What could she do now? And most important, where was Rene?

Daphne abruptly stood up and brushed the dust from her skirt. She couldn't continue to sit there helplessly. She decided to put Coral in the stable behind the house and give her some oats.

Glad to have something to do, Daphne led the horse to the stables and set about finding a feedbag.

"What are you doing in here?" A high-pitched voice sounded behind her. Daphne spun around to find herself confronted by a thin, dark-haired woman pointing a pistol at her. With a startled cry, Daphne backed away.

"I came to see Miss Drummond," she stammered, "but there's no one home, so I brought my horse in here."

"You stole that horse from her?" the woman asked suspiciously.

"Oh, no! Coral is mine. I'm a teacher here," added Daphne, hoping to mollify the woman. The declaration had the desired effect. The woman lowered the pistol.

"Where is Miss Drummond?" asked Daphne, and the woman stared at her in surprise. "Where is everyone?" cried Daphne, panic mounting.

"Haven't you heard?"

"No!" shouted Daphne. "Tell me, please."

"She's gone to try to stop it."

"To stop who? What's going on?" A wave of fear engulfed Daphne. Had something happened to Rene?

"A lot of our men are dead. The Philadelphia militia shot thirty of them. Swine." The woman spat on the floor.

Daphne swayed. Rene! Was he hurt? What was

the Philadelphia militia doing here? Why were they shooting people? What had Rene or Miss Drummond to do with it?

"Where is Miss Drummond?"

"At the railway depot. The roundhouse. There is a mob there and the people want to avenge their brothers. They will kill the militia if they can."

Daphne ran from the stable, her reticule swinging from her arm. She had to get to the depot to find Lilleth. She would know if Rene was all right.

Out on the street, Daphne forced herself to run faster. She rounded a corner and found herself in the park in front of the railway depot and roundhouse. The square was packed with people, hundreds of people, shoulder to shoulder, men, women, and children shouting at the tops of their voices. Many held guns. Daphne's eyes widened with fear and she started at the popping sounds of the shots. The militiamen in the roundhouse were shooting at the crowd! Screams echoed through the roar of the mob.

Daphne stood, unable to move. How could she hope to find Lilleth or Rene in this sea of people? She pushed her way slowly through the mass of people, searching desperately for Rene. Each time she caught sight of a dark head of wavy hair above broad shoulders, she caught her breath, hope surging wildly through her. But it was never Rene and she saw no sign of Lilleth.

Reaching the front of the crowd, Daphne could see that the mob had surrounded the roundhouse. The soldiers were trapped inside. People in the crowd without guns had picked up paving stones and were hurling them at the roundhouse. Those with guns fired at the windows of the roundhouse. Daphne knew she was in danger, but she would not leave until she found either Rene or Lilleth.

Daphne's heart chilled at the sights and sounds around her. What could have happened to have caused this fury? Some dreadful lot of killing had caused the mob's blood lust. Next to her a man fell wounded, dropping his gun. Another picked up the weapon and raised it to his shoulder. He aimed and shot at the soldiers.

"I avenge my brother," he shouted as he fired.

Just then an enormous explosion shook the ground. The mob had found a cannon and had managed to drag it to the scene. The cannonball had knocked a hole in the front of the roundhouse. The crowd cheered as soldiers streamed out the back of the building.

The crowd fired after the retreating soldiers, but did not chase them. There was no need to. They had made their point and the militia had run away.

Another louder explosion sounded from the building. Powder kegs inside the roundhouse exploded, setting fire to the building and causing more kegs to explode.

Panic gripped the crowd as acrid smoke billowed forth from the flaming building. The fire took only seconds to spread through the building. The roof caved in with a sickening crackle and the tongues of flame devoured the shell of the roundhouse, reaching out toward the buildings on either side of it.

People screamed, pushing against one another, desperate to get away from the fire. Daphne began to choke as she inhaled smoke. It was all she could do to stay on her feet as the mob surged around her. At last the wind shifted and blew the smoke away from the crowd. Daphne caught her breath in deep gasps, turned away, and with a mighty effort, pushed through the crowd, away from the square.

As she began to calm down a little, Daphne caught sight of a dark head just a few feet away from her and her heart lurched.

"Rene!" she shouted through parched lips.

The man did not move or respond. Daphne's head drooped in sorrow. She had been mistaken once more.

"Daphne!" cried his voice, his face registering disbelief.

He was alive! Daphne was flooded with inexpressible joy. She stretched one hand forward to try to reach him and they struggled toward one another, their hands outstretched. It seemed that they would never reach one another, that the crowd would keep them apart forever.

Rene looked raptly at Daphne's grime-smeared face and her tangled hair. Suddenly a movement behind Daphne caught his eye.

A large, heavyset man was moving purposefully toward her, tipping a small vial into a handkerchief. Rene's fists clenched in rage as he struggled more feverishly to reach Daphne before the stranger did. His eyes widened in horror as the thug grabbed Daphne from behind and pressed the obviously chloroform-soaked handkerchief to her face. She slumped into his arms, not even aware of what had happened.

Rene yelled in fury. He shoved against the people who separated him from Daphne. There was nothing he could do. He was trapped by the crowd and could only witness Daphne's kidnapping. It was like some dreadful nightmare only worse, for Rene knew that this was reality. A scream of rage and frustration issued from some inner depth of his soul. The crowd began to move again and it swept Rene towards the spot where Daphne had been standing when she had been abducted. *Daphne*, he silently cried. *Oh, Daphne, I almost reached you.*

Daphne groaned and wondered vaguely where she was. For a moment she couldn't remember where she had been or what she had been doing. Rene's face swam before her eyes, but it had an expression of terror on it. Daphne opened her eyes and looked around.

What an odd place to be, she thought groggily. This is the old storage closet. I must have come in here for something and fallen down.

Daphne stood up unsteadily and tried the door handle. It wouldn't open! She sat down on a trunk to try to figure out what had happened.

She looked down with surprise at her blackened hands and arms. Slowly, the day's events began to come back to Daphne and she recalled how she had run from the house to search for Rene. She had almost reached him, but something had happened. But what? Daphne couldn't understand what she was doing back in her father's house and why she was locked in a closet.

Suddenly the door opened and Elspeth's stern face looked in. She was dressed in a short cloak and bonnet over a traveling gown.

"So you're awake. We're ready for you now, you little minx."

Elspeth grasped Daphne roughly by the arm and half-dragged her into one of the spare bedrooms, where a steaming pitcher of water stood beside a wash basin. Elspeth sat down to watch as though her niece were a prisoner and she her jailer.

Too startled to protest at the treatment she was receiving, Daphne removed the top of her dress and washed her face and arms carefully.

"Put that on," said Elspeth coldly, pointing to a dress laid out on the bed. It was also a traveling suit. Where was she going?

Daphne dressed slowly, her mind racing, trying to buy time to decide what to do now.

"Hurry up," commanded her aunt. "Now brush out your hair and put it up. No primping, you little harlot." Elspeth set her lips in a thin line of disapproval.

Finally Daphne was dressed to Elspeth's satisfaction. Elspeth beckoned to Daphne and together they descended the stairs. Daphne's father stood at the bottom, his arms folded across his chest.

"Everything is ready. The carriage is waiting and her things are all loaded," Jeb said to Elspeth.

Elspeth took Daphne more firmly by the arm and led her toward the door.

"Wait!" cried Daphne. "Where are you taking me?"

"You are going to Paris to live with my sister Isabel for the time being," answered her father.

"But why?"

"You shameless hussy," hissed Elspeth.

"Be quiet, Elspeth," said Jeb. "You know what you've done. You have formed an unfortunate attachment to a person far beneath you. You are betrothed to another. You'll go to Paris and live with Isabel until we have disposed of this person and then you'll come back and marry Caleb."

"No! No! I'm going to marry Rene. I won't marry anyone else," cried Daphne, stricken.

"You'll do as you're told," replied Jeb. "Right now I want you to get into the carriage or we'll use the chloroform again."

Daphne found herself in the carriage, traveling rapidly out of the city toward New York and a ship to Paris. Her mind was reeling from all the recent events.

Chapter 15

Heddie plodded down the road toward Bayardstown, exhausted from her day's work at the Slater mansion. She was deeply worried about Daphne and saddened that her friend had been so cruelly wrenched away from her.

"Psssst," someone called from the side of the road. Heddie stopped in surprise and looked cautiously about her.

"Who's there?" she asked.

Rene LeBrun stepped out from behind a small grouping of trees and said softly, "Keep on walking normally, Heddie. I must know what's happened to Daphne, and yet I can't be seen talking to you."

Shocked by his sudden appearance, Heddie took a few seconds to get the words out. "They won't let me talk about it at the house, but I have a feeling that Miss Elspeth is keeping me employed so that I won't speak of her niece outside the Slater house. Oh, Rene, Daphne has disappeared! I am afraid . . .," here she paused, glancing nervously at him, hesitant to cause him sorrow.

"I'm afraid that Daphne has been sent to Paris. I think that's what I overheard yesterday afternoon. But I can't be sure. Her father and aunt were talking so fast and I still have trouble with English. And they were behind a closed door. But I heard arguing and I know I heard 'Paris.' One of the maids said Daphne has been sent to live with her aunt. She didn't want to go, Rene. No one says anything about her coming back! Oh, Rene!"

His face had gone white. What could she do to make it easier? Heddie thought frantically. If only she might repay Daphne's kindness by helping Rene now.

"I've lost her for good," Rene said in a flat, emotionless voice. "They'll seduce her away from me with bright lights and the thrill of Paris. I guess it's for the best. What kind of life could she have had with me? She'd have come to hate it and despise me." After a long silence he continued, "My duty is here, helping the organizers and strikers. I shouldn't think of personal happiness. Yes, it's best that she's gone," he said in a hard voice. "She'll soon forget me," he whispered bitterly. But his heart cried out, *Daphne ... Daphne.*

Strikes in Baltimore by railway workers who refused to accept the longer hours and lower wages decreed by management had set off similar strikes across the country. Pittsburgh strikes were especially violent. Crowds of angry workers roamed the streets, gathering around the rail yards, shouting. The Pittsburgh militia was called out, but the men refused to fight against their brothers. The governor of Pennsylvania called in the Philadelphia militia and later, federal troops, to put down the strike.

When the militia arrived on July 21, 1877, its first action was to arrest the strike leaders. A crowd formed around their leaders and the militia fired into the unruly mob, killing twenty-nine people and wounding many more. The enraged mob chased the militia back to the railway line. The militiamen took refuge in the roundhouse and the crowd, now armed, began to fire on the militia. At last a cannon was brought out and fired at the roundhouse, vanquishing the soldiers. The delirious mob wanted further revenge against the soldiers and the railroad, both for the men who had died in the first skirmish and for the fifty more who had fallen in the battle outside the roundhouse. Thus came about the torching of the roundhouse and the great fire Daphne had witnessed. In the four days that followed, mob rule reigned in Pittsburgh to be put down only by armed vigilante committees and federal troops. The ringleaders of the strike were arrested and given long jail sentences. A few days later the governor himself arrived to re-open the lines—the railroads were moving again.

Having at least outwardly accepted Daphne's disappearance from his life, Rene threw himself into labor organizing. He would not allow himself to think about his lost love. Rene was in full sympathy with his fellow workers' wage demands, for he well knew the hardships under which they were already suffering from the paltry wages they were paid. But he could not agree with the tactics of mob violence. The men had to be brought under control, the killing had to be stopped, for it would bring only more violence.

Rene did not work alone. Lilleth Drummond was by his side, as was Robert A. Ammons, leader of the strikers.

Their days were endlessly frustrating. No one could control the mob, not even its brothers in the labor movement. At this point only a superior force could stop the enraged masses roaming Pittsburgh, burning down buildings, overturning railway cars, and looting railway property.

Caleb Winters, Jeb Slater and the other leaders of industry were by no means idle during the four days of riots. They were planning their strategy to crush the labor movement and to use the rioting as an excuse for arresting all the labor leaders in Pittsburgh.

"This riot may be a Godsend for us, Jeb," Caleb stated. "The rioting will help us to get rid of all those damn agitators. That'll also help to keep prices down."

"Yes," answered Jeb with relish, "and we'll be able to do away with that Rene LeBrun. Do you think he can be hung for his part in this disgraceful business?"

"He's a cautious devil and the courts are soft, but there's every reason to hope. Yes, he'll be out of our way soon. But why are you so interested in him specifically?"

"Just that we discussed what to do about him once before," said Jeb, hoping that Caleb wouldn't notice that he was lying. Caleb must never learn about Daphne's relations with Rene or all chance of their marriage would be finished! "You know I've sent Daphne off to stay with my sister Isabel in Paris until this business blows over."

"But it'll be a matter of days. Her boat will still

be in port by the time we have these rascals crying for mercy."

"Well . . . she was looking a bit peaked. And Paris life will polish her, make her grow a bit." Jeb chuckled heartily and then changed the subject.

July twenty-sixth dawned hot and muggy. Men's tempers flared and blazed as hot as the fires burning in the rail yards. Early that morning, as the mob surged out into the streets, they were met by armed men on horseback—Pinkerton agents, mine owners, the industry kingpins. Behind them were the militia, also heavily armed. The crowd was no match for such an army and they melted back as the soldiers advanced on them, clubbing the stragglers with the butts of their guns.

The afternoon remained hot, but the town was silent. People were afraid to leave their houses because the militia were patrolling the streets, stopping anyone who was walking about, their guns much in evidence.

Rene went to his room in the settlement house and threw himself down on his narrow cot. He buried his face in his arms and shut his eyes. The past four days of rioting had been an endless endurance test and there had been no time for sleep. Rene had not wanted to rest anyway, for rest meant thoughts of Daphne and the torment of knowing that their love was over. He shut his eyes tightly, hoping to block out Daphne's image.

The door flew open, banging on its hinges. "You're under arrest," shouted a voice. Rough hands seized him. Rene LeBrun didn't know it yet, but Jeb

Slater and Caleb Winters had accomplished his removal to prison—each for his own reasons.

The chill sea breeze blew off the grey waters of New York harbor as Daphne stood at the stern of the ship, sadly watching the great city disappear. She stared fixedly at the muddy water, her thoughts far away.

Memories of the hasty journey from Pittsburgh to Philadelphia and then to New York filled her mind. With each mile, she had traveled farther away from Rene and from happiness. But she had been helpless to stop her journey. At first she had tried to protest, to reason with Elsepth and her father, but soon she knew the effort was useless. Later she had resigned herself to her destiny and sank wan and exhausted into a stupor.

"You must come in now," said Letty appearing at her shoulder with a warm cloak. "We've lost sight of the shore already and the captain tells me there's rough water ahead."

Daphne nodded mechanically, her fingers stroking the soft black cashmere cloak that had so recently covered her as she and Rene lay in the sheltering woods.

"Ah, you'll get over him," Letty soothed, smiling indulgently, for Mr. Slater had told her nearly everything.

"Never," cried Daphne. "Never. I'll love him as long as I live."

The next two days were stormy, and Letty and Daphne were confined to their cabin, so sick that each thought she would die. For two days, the ship rolled and shuddered with each massive wave, its engines throbbing uselessly as it attempted to make headway.

The third day of their voyage dawned clear. Daphne managed to find her legs and went up on deck, pale and weakened, for some fresh air. After two days of constant retching, she managed to walk only as far as the railing, and she clung to it for a few minutes, trying to gain enough strength to walk into the dining room.

"*Avez-vous besoin d'assistance?*" A male voice sounded at her elbow. It was a deep, resonant voice.

Before Daphne could collect herself enough to respond in French, the man took her arm and escorted her in to breakfast.

"You are American, yes?" Daphne nodded. "I guessed correctly, then, eh?" continued the tall, elegantly dressed dark-haired man.

"But I thought you were French! Are you English?" stammered Daphne as they seated themselves.

The man laughed. "You flatter me. My English is not as good as all that. I was educated at Oxford and have just come back from a two-year tour of your country. But I am forgetting my manners. Allow me to present myself, Aristide Auguste Romain de la Tour, at your service," he said, rising, then bowing to her across the table. Daphne could almost hear his heels click.

"My, what a long name," noted Daphne, obviously impressed. "I'm just Daphne Slater."

"You have a tragic past? You seem very sad."

Daphne leaned forward across the small table and whispered, "I'm being sent to Paris against my will." Aristide made a sympathetic noise. "To live with a dreadful maiden aunt. I lived with another one in Pittsburgh, that's where I'm from, but I expect this one will be even worse."

"Mon Dieu!" exclaimed Aristide. Daphne didn't know what it meant, but it had a nice sound to it. "Tell me more."

Daphne blushed. "I have a lover and my family doesn't approve of him. We were to run away and be married. But then there was a riot and someone told my father about us and then he had me kidnapped." Daphne's eyes widened. "I was chloroformed."

"Frightful business, I must say," interjected Aristide. "But your 'lover,' he could do nothing to prevent this?"

"Oh, no. Absolutely nothing." Daphne took a large bite of the sweet roll on the plate in front of her.

"But why has he not followed you, if I may ask?"

"My father said he would be put in jail. That may be where Rene is right now. I tried to escape myself, but my Aunt Elspeth was watching me like a hawk."

Daphne was struck by the thought that as she sat in a nicely decorated dining salon on board a pleasantly rocking ship, Rene most probably was languishing in a damp, horrid prison. A twinge of conscience shot through her heart and Daphne hastily excused herself and fled to her cabin.

"I shan't go out anymore. I don't want to meet that Frenchman. What right have I to laugh and be happy while Rene is a prisoner, sick and miserable?"

Aristide remained at their table for some time after Daphne had left. He stared off into space and smiled to himself, aimlessly twisting his mustache.

"She *is* like a princess in a fairy story. Just now she ran off like Cinderella at the stroke of midnight. Such a piquant, amusing little thing. And so pretty despite those dreadful American clothes. But dressed as a Parisienne, she will outshine all Paris. A beauty, and that hair! Magnifique. I am sure I should make the acquaintance of her French aunt." Aristide laughed softly to himself and called the waiter over to ascertain the name of the pretty Cinderella and the address in Paris where she would be staying. On hearing it, his eyebrows lifted.

Montmartre! To Aristide, the word Montmartre conjured up a world of Bohemian artists, of absinthe drinkers, of the little grisettes who roamed the streets in search of love—for pay.

This little flower may be available. Perhaps one could enter into negotiations? Still, one never knows, these Americans are so often eccentric. He sighed.

Daphne stayed as far away from Aristide as possible for the rest of the voyage. She feared the intimacy that had sprung up so quickly between them. She was pledged to Rene and vowed to remain true to him.

Aristide did not press her. You and I will meet again soon, and I'll make you happy, he thought. I know how to break down a woman's reserve. Aristide smiled to himself.

When Daphne and Letty arrived in Calais, Daphne scanned the crowd that clustered around the edge of the dock waiting for the dinghies to bring their friends in from the great ship docked out in the harbor. She was searching for a stiff, starched, precise copy of Aunt Elspeth. Nowhere did she find such a person in the crowd. Daphne sighed. Aunt Isabel must have sent a servant to fetch her rather than come all the way from Paris herself.

Daphne's eye was caught by a lady dressed in an Oriental costume of rich reds and purples, a lime-green fez cocked precariously over one extravagantly kohled eye. She was not Oriental, however. A lavish flood of faded blonde curls coursed down her back. This shocking apparition caught sight of Daphne, stared intently at her and then rushed forward to wrap her in an embrace.

"Daphne, my child," the woman crowed. "I would have known you anywhere. You look so like your dear mother—and, of course, you have my hair. Now what have you done that was so bad my foolish brother had to send you to me?"

"Aunt Isabel?" queried Daphne timorously, astonished.

"Ah, I see they've been careful to tell you nothing about me," Isabel Slater said wryly. "I suppose you imagined someone more like Elspeth?"

Daphne nodded. "But I'm glad you're not like her," she said impulsively, warming instantly to the bizarre woman standing before her.

"Now, why have Jeb and Elspeth sent you here? Their telegrams were brief and told me nothing. They claimed it was for your health, but you look well enough to me. Anyway, for that they could have sent you to Sarasota. Now, out with it. We may as well be frank with one another."

"I wanted to marry Rene and they kidnapped me and sent me here."

"I thought it might be something of that kind. And why don't they like Rene?"

"He's a coal miner and a labor organizer and is poor. And also they want me to marry a man I detest. Caleb Winters, who's a mine owner."

"That is a difficult situation," sighed Isabel. "Still, as long as you're here, you and I might as well enjoy our visit. I'll show you Paris and you and I can get to know one another."

"Aunt Isabel, I'm determined to escape and return to Rene," Daphne announced. "Rene may be in jail right now."

"In jail? My, my, the story gets worse and worse. But come, you can tell me all about it on the way to Paris," Isabel said, dismissing the subject. "Now say good-bye to your maid." Letty was returning on the next ship, there being no need for her in Paris.

Isabel waited as Letty and Daphne bid one another a tearful farewell. Then the aunt and niece settled in Isabel's coach and were on their way to Paris. "By the by, who was that handsome Frenchman staring at you?" asked her aunt.

Daphne blushed. "Aristide Auguste Romain de la Tour."

"Ooh la la! You *have* made a conquest. He is one of the richest men in Paris, and from one of the city's oldest families. But I hear he is quite the rake. He had to be sent off to America after killing a man in a duel over a prostitute. Still, for all his reputation, Aristide is an eligible bachelor."

Daphne's ears burned. Duels! Prostitutes! Life with this aunt would not be dull.

Chapter 16

Daphne awoke to the mingled smells of strong coffee brewing and turpentine. She stretched in the large, high bed and surveyed the room. She had arrived too late the night before to form any impression of the place Aunt Isabel had brought her to.

A profusion of Oriental paintings hung on the walls. Small moroccon leather ottomans were placed around the floor and in one corner sat a smiling green Buddha. These Eastern relics contrasted with the massive antique bed Daphne was sleeping in and the huge mahogany armoire that took up most of one wall. She got out of bed and ran over to the window to open the shutters and get her first glimpse of Paris by day.

Daphne's room overlooked the inner courtyard of the building. Rows of clotheslines held flapping white linen. The walls were whitewashed. A battery of housemaids were beating rugs against the walls as they gossiped.

"Planning your escape already?" Isabel inquired, sneaking up behind Daphne. "It's six stories down, so I really think escaping from that window is hopeless."

Daphne turned round with a smile and then stared, taking in her aunt's costume. "But you're wearing pants!" exclaimed Daphne before she could stop herself.

Isabel giggled. "Yes, I generally do around the house. They're so comfortable." Isabel pirouetted to show off her costume. Very full harem-style pants in purple velvet with a green and gold paisley pattern were gathered at the ankles. Leather slippers with curled up toes, a flowing pink chemise and a short red velvet jacket encrusted with gold beadwork and mirrors added to the extraordinary outfit.

"My, but you have a lot of unusual things!" exclaimed Daphne.

"Yes, I do. I've traveled quite a lot in the East and I always seem to bring back trunks filled with exotic garb. The Eastern sense of color is extraordinary, don't you think?" Daphne nodded, not quite sure what to say to all this.

"Put this on and we'll go in to breakfast," continued Isabel, tossing a brightly colored Japanese kimono at Daphne. Daphne put on the silky orange and purple garment and admired herself in the mirror.

"I can see why you like to wear these clothes, Aunt Isabel."

Isabel led Daphne through the large high-ceilinged rooms of the apartment, each one more strangely furnished than the last, to a small terrace overlooking the city. They ate their breakfast on the terrace, screened by potted palm trees.

"Oh, Paris is lovely," breathed Daphne. "It looks so French. All those mazes of streets and the cobbles and so much activity! Why, it's bigger than Pittsburgh, but there's no coal dust in the air. And the river; how beautiful! And all those churches. Why, I can see Notre Dame. What a wonderful place." Daphne took a deep breath of the summer air, trying to take in Paris with all her senses.

Isabel smiled at her fondly, glad to see her niece happy. She had been worried by Daphne's sad story. A young woman pining for her lost love would be a difficult guest to amuse. Isabel hoped to convince the girl that enjoying life would not be a betrayal of Rene.

Daphne sat down at the table with Isabel, her hunger having won over her curiosity to see Paris. An appealing assortment of soft puffy rolls were laid in a basket and Daphne chose and bit into one.

"Delicious," she exclaimed, her mouth full. "What's it called?"

"A croissant," answered Isabel, smiling at her niece's appetite.

"That's awfully funny-looking gruel, if you don't mind my saying so." Daphne pointed to a deep bowl of coffee-colored liquid. Picking up her spoon with an air of resignation, she tentatively sipped the nasty-looking stuff.

Isabel laughed. "That's not gruel, that's coffee. The French drink it out of big bowls like that in the morning. *Café au lait.*"

"So that's the wonderful smell that woke me up. But why do I smell turpentine?"

"I am afraid you'll always smell turpentine in this

house. Didn't Jeb and Elspeth tell you that I am a painter?"

"No," answered Daphne truthfully, for they never had told her anything at all about this strange but fantastic aunt.

"Old wounds don't heal," remarked Isabel, her face sad. "I'll tell you my story, Daphne. Basically, I was much in your position once, not because I had fallen in love with someone unsuitable, but because *I* was someone unsuitable. I wanted to be an artist. In trying to learn my craft, I became a scandal.

"It all happened long before you were born. It seems rather silly now, but at the time it was devastating. Painting was all I cared about for many years, and no one minded. It seemed a harmless enough diversion for a young girl. Only it wasn't a diversion for me, it was everything. I wanted terribly to learn how to be a great painter. So, I went to a drawing class dressed as a man. It was, you understand, an anatomy drawing class.

"No one in the class was fooled by my disguise, of course, but they could pretend to be fooled. That allowed them to admit me to the class. Things went well until my family discovered what I'd been doing. In no time, all Pittsburgh was a-buzz with the story. Imagine," she mimicked bitterly, "Isabel Slater going to a class to look at naked men and women. And dressed as a man! People stopped speaking to me. I was no longer respectable. The family was incensed. So they sent me to Paris with an allowance and got rid of me. Better for all of us, really," Isabel concluded.

"But how cruel of them!" cried Daphne.

"I don't suppose they meant to be cruel. They are

all rather narrow people and I had violated their code. Your mother was the only person who stood by me through all of it. Well . . . it was a long time ago. Now I am happy, and a far better artist for living in Paris instead of Pittsburgh. Come, I'll show you my studio."

Isabel led Daphne up a narrow flight of steps to a large, untidy attic room. The windows faced north. On a table in one corner was a still life of fruits and glasses. In the center of the room was a raised platform for a model to pose on. Canvases were stacked against the walls. The paintings were like nothing Daphne had ever seen. They had a rapid, unfinished quality about them, a brightness and vigor that made them seem alive. The paint was laid on in thick, hurried strokes as though Isabel had been trying to capture the essence of life itself.

"I've never seen anything like them," breathed Daphne. "They're beautiful. They're almost alive."

She stared at an unfinished work set on an easel facing the model's platform. The painting was of a nearly naked blonde woman, her hair tangled and fair, her flesh rosy. She stared candidly out at the viewer, a strong air of magnetism and sexuality about her. Daphne was entranced.

"I see you, too, have fallen in love with Nana. All of Paris has, so you needn't be ashamed. She's a wonderful creature, a magnificent animal. She's an actress, not to mention the mistress of one of the most powerful men in France."

Daphne blushed and lowered her gaze.

"Oh, dear, I've shocked you! You're not used to such open talk, are you? I wasn't either when I came here."

For the next month, Isabel and Daphne went around Paris together, visiting the historic churches and roaming for hours through the museums. Paris seemed strangely quiet and Isabel told Daphne that was because everyone left the city to spend August in the country. After two weeks in the city, sightseeing and buying a new, modish wardrobe, Daphne and Isabel left for two weeks in the country.

After a brief but relaxing stay in the French countryside, they returned to Paris. Daphne accompanied her aunt on a bewildering whirl of parties, gallery openings and soirees. During the day, Isabel locked herself in her attic room and painted, but at night and in the late afternoons, she was free to go out.

Daphne spent her days wandering from room to room, thinking of Rene. She read sometimes and tried to improve her French by talking with the maids. She wrote long letters to her beloved and sent them to the settlement house with instructions to Lilleth Drummond to forward them to Rene, wherever he was. She also wrote to Lilleth asking for any news of Rene.

If Daphne's days were sad and lonely, her nights were busy and bewildering. Isabel took Daphne with her wherever she went. Her friends were odder even than she was. She knew all the famous artists and writers in Paris and visited them in their studios or in the cafes they enjoyed. Daphne often felt uncomfortable with these artists, for she understood their language imperfectly and found their conversations about art were out of her territory. Furthermore, she found their talk about life shocking.

One day Isabel said, "I think you aren't happy

here with me. You're thin and pale and I think you often cry late into the night. I'm going to write to your father and ask if I can send you home."

"I'm not unhappy with you, Aunt Isabel. It's just that I miss Rene. And I worry about him all the time. He may be in jail or even . . . dead." Daphne began to sob and Isabel took her in her arms and tried to comfort her.

"Why should he be dead?"

"They may have hung him. Papa and Caleb were trying to get evidence against him, all false, but the court would believe it and sentence him to death." Daphne's sobs renewed themselves as she imagined Rene on his way to the gallows.

"You don't know for sure what has happened to him. He may be just fine. You don't know."

"But I haven't heard from him, and I've written to our friend Lilleth, and she hasn't answered. I'd rather stay here, though, even with all my worrying. If I go back, Papa said he'd make me marry Caleb."

"Whatever you wish, Daphne. You're welcome to stay. I only want you to be happy."

Daphne and Isabel went out into the warm September evening, the sky a less intense blue now that the sun was setting. The odor of absinthe, the thick green liqueur that was so potent it could cause death, hung over Montmartre as it did every day at dusk. They were on their way to Edouard Manet's house for a small party in his studio.

"I always love to see Edouard. Such a brilliant man! And today he'll show us what he's been painting over the summer. I'm sure you'll enjoy meeting him, Daphne, and there should be lots of interesting people at his party." Isabel smiled happily at the prospect of the long hours to come of artistic discussion. Daphne nodded and straightened the bustle at the back of her black skirt. She rather doubted that the people at the party would be interesting.

Manet's studio was much like the studios of other artists. The furniture was of a better quality because his paintings sold well. Edouard Manet was quite nice. Daphne walked around the room, leaving her aunt lost in admiration of a large painting of the countryside in the south of France. In Daphne's opinion, this was the best part of any soiree. No one expected you to express opinions and theories about the paintings. You could just look at them, become lost in their beauty. Too soon, however, that part of the evening was over and the party split up into groups. Everyone chattered happily about the work he had done over the summer and the new galleries that had opened. Daphne wandered into a corner and amused herself by playing with Manet's cat.

A commotion near the door attracted her attention. It was as though everyone in the room had gasped. A woman entered. All eyes turned to stare at her, mesmerized. Suddenly Manet remembered that he was the host and cried, "Nana! Welcome!" Conversations then resumed, but with a difference. Now everyone was terribly aware of the woman.

From her corner, Daphne had ample opportunity to stare at Nana unobserved. She was very beautiful, but that was not what made her so arresting. Daphne was not sure what it was. She seemed knowing in some way, assured that everyone would be impressed by her. She knew she was powerful.

Nana wore a very simple dark pink gown, cut

low in the bosom and without sleeves. Her shoulders and arms glowed, seeming to give off an almost golden light. When she laughed she threw back her head, revealing white teeth and a very pink tongue.

"What do you think of me, *chérie?* I see you looking at me," remarked Nana, walking swiftly over to Daphne.

Daphne blushed. "I'm sorry, I shouldn't have stared." Nana reached out and touched Daphne's cheek.

"Like a rose," she murmured.

"I was thinking that my aunt has caught you very well in the portrait she is doing of you."

Nana laughed. "Ah, you are the niece of *chère* Isabel. Then you are of my family! I would rather sit for Isabel than for anyone." Daphne basked in the warmth and affection that Nana exuded.

"You will come to see me perform soon, yes? I want Isabel to bring you. My new play opens soon at the opera house. It is not dull, unlike these dreadful parties." Nana adopted a conspiratorial tone and leaned so close to Daphne that she could smell her lilac scent. "I come only so they all will paint me and I'll become more famous. It's good for business, *chérie.*" Nana laughed. "We will meet again soon, but now I must be off to pamper these old fools and make them want to paint me more than anything else in the world."

Nana flitted off, leaving Daphne just a little stunned. It was incredible that this wonderful creature should want to meet her again. Daphne sighed. Nana was so lovely and fresh, and yet, there was something earthy about her. Daphne could not quite understand it.

The new Paris opera house was a grand stone palace, glowing with the light from the gas jets within. It presided majestically over the Place de l'Opéra. Daphne had seen it by day, but she had not realized how splendid it would be at night.

Daphne and her aunt swept up the long flight of marble steps that led to the main entrance. There was a terrible crush as gentlemen entered the theater with ladies in beautiful gowns and jewels, their hair artfully arranged either crowning their heads or cascading in curls down their backs. An overwhelming smell of flowers and perfume hung in the hot, still night air.

As she entered the opera house, Daphne felt like Cinderella on her way to the ball. This was as beautiful as any of her old daydreams. Why all around her were princes and counts!

As Daphne and Isabel rounded a corner, Daphne saw two well-dressed, light-haired women coming toward them. The older of the two was slightly past her prime, and must once have been very beautiful. She was tall and majestic-looking, wearing a richly patterned satin gown in black and gold. The young girl wore a white voile dress in the latest fashion. How pretty she is, thought Daphne, and in that moment she realized she was looking at a reflection of herself and Isabel in the full-length mirror at the top of the steps.

Daphne and Isabel made their way to their box. All the people were so beautiful and wore such magnificent clothes and jewels. The crowd hummed with excitement, for Nana was a great favorite. At last the lights went down, the orchestra began to play, and the red velvet curtains swung open.

The sets were elaborate and beautiful and were often changed as parts of the stage shifted to and fro to reveal new scenery. Daphne was spellbound. She had often been to the theater in Pittsburgh, but it never had been anything like this. The curtains closed, signaling the end of the first act. Still, Nana had not appeared on stage.

During the intermission, Daphne and Isabel remained in their box, observing the rest of the audience. Isabel kept up a running commentary, telling Daphne who various members of the audience were and explaining their relationships to one another.

"Ah, Daphne, there's your beau from the boat, Aristide de la Tour." She passed Daphne the opera glasses and Daphne looked to where he was sitting. He was as handsome as she remembered, more so now that he wore formal dress. "And look who he's with!" Isabel exclaimed. "Celine."

Daphne looked at the woman beside Aristide as Isabel continued her discourse. She was a raven-haired beauty, her skin very white and creamy, wearing a red dress that seemed shot with fire. At her throat was a magnificent diamond that seemed to wink at Daphne from across the theater.

Suddenly she felt Aristide's eyes upon her, looking deep into her heart. She remained caught in his gaze for a long moment and then turned abruptly toward Isabel, feigning disinterest and making rapid conversation.

The lights dimmed for the second act and for a few moments Daphne felt a vague sense of guilt as she recalled the emotions she had experienced when Aristide had looked at her. What had happened to her?

The curtains swung open once again to reveal Nana, standing nearly naked in a *tableau vivant*. She remained perfectly still for a moment as the crowd drank in her beauty. The audience followed the rest of the act with tremendous interest, for while Nana was not a great actress, she was an extraordinary performer and enthralled the audience.

After the last curtain call, the lights went up and the crowd buzzed with excitement. Nana was a sensation! "Oh, Aunt Isabel, thank you for bringing me! It was wonderful," cried Daphne.

"Odd, but I no longer find the plays as interesting as I find the audience," mused Isabel. "I must be growing old. You know, de la Tour must be taken with Celine or he would not have parted with one of his family's finest jewels. You saw the diamond? I wonder what he sees in her, for she is as cold and unscrupulous as she is beautiful. Ah, well, there is no telling. Come, Daphne, we must pay our compliments to Nana or she will pretend never to forgive us."

All Paris seemed to have gone backstage to congratulate Nana. Actresses in short, full skirts rushed to their dressing rooms and young men bearing enormous bouquets of flowers followed them, begging to be allowed to speak if they had not been introduced, caressing them fondly if they were well acquainted. Many people were rushing toward Nana's door, anxious to see her after her great triumph.

"We'll never get past that crush," observed Isabel. "We'll have to send her flowers and chocolates tomorrow, I am afraid."

Terribly disappointed, Daphne turned sadly away.

"*Chérie*," cried a familiar voice. Nana poked her

head out of her dressing room. "I cannot see you now because all these tiresome creatures are here. But soon I will come to see you and we will have a lovely gossip."

"You were so wonderful. A jewel! Oh, I never saw anything like it," Daphne called to her. "I'll see you soon."

Daphne walked out of the theater barely noticing her surroundings, for she had been deeply affected by the glamour of the stage.

Chapter 17

Daphne was awakened by the maid, who arrived bearing an enormous bouquet of cut flowers. Daphne sniffed the flowers eagerly, admiring the yellow snapdragons, the crimson spears of gladiolus. Handing them back to the maid to be put on her bedside table, Daphne tore open the accompanying card.

You are more beautiful than ever.

Devotedly, an admirer.

Daphne was stunned. Could Aristide have sent them? It had to be him. Who else would do such a thing?

At the breakfast table that morning Isabel said, "I understand that you received an enormous bouquet. Who is your admirer? Is it Aristide de la Tour?"

Daphne explained about the unsigned card.

"I'm not sure I like this. What will we do now?" Isabel wondered. Daphne looked up, startled. "He'll want to make your acquaintance and I'm not sure that that is wise."

"But why not?" asked Daphne before she could stop herself. "I mean, I don't want to see him. He's nothing to me. I'm only curious."

"You are very young, Daphne, and you don't know what a man like that would try to do to you. He would trifle with you and make you unhappy. No, he is unsuitable for you, much too fast. We must rebuff any advances. Be on your guard," Isabel's stern tone sobered her niece considerably.

"I don't care for him in the least, you know. Rene has my heart."

"Yes, but you are so young and Rene is so far away. In the three months you have been here he has not written," Isabel pointed out as gently as she could.

Daphne shook her head stubbornly and left the room, angry with Isabel for suggesting that she could ever forget Rene.

Daphne and Nana were walking arm in arm in the Jardins du Luxembourg on a mild, late October morning. The sun shone brightly but there was a distinct autumn feeling in the air. The trees had already begun to take on russet tones and the first leaves were falling.

"I'm always sad to see the summer go," Nana said wistfully. "I love the hot weather, the feel of the warm air against my skin. Ah, summer."

"I had such hopes for this summer," Daphne sighed forlornly.

"You are too young for such sadness. Life holds everything for you. There is love to come."

"Not for me," answered Daphne. "I have buried my heart."

Nana clicked her tongue impatiently.

Impulsively, Daphne told Nana all about herself and Rene, and their star-crossed romance.

"How tragic, how sad," Nana murmured stroking Daphne's arm as they sat on a park bench. She was surprised by the girl's story. "I feel for you, *chérie*, but you will find other loves and be happy again."

Daphne shook her head. "I could never love anyone else. I have given my very soul to Rene."

The two were silent for a few moments, each feeling that the other had failed to understand. In the week since Daphne had seen Nana at the opera, the two women had walked together in the park each morning before lunch. There was a strong sense of kinship and harmony between them, and this disagreement was awkward. They were both quite lonely and had come to depend upon one another for empathy. Daphne had no friends of her own age in Paris, of course, and Nana, though she had many lovers, had no true friends.

"Ah, *chérie*, let us not disagree. I shall believe in the beauty of your love. It is just that my own experience has been so different," said Nana, kissing Daphne's cheek to settle the argument.

Soon they were walking happily about the park, chattering gaily. In the sunlight they looked like sisters, both fair and equally beautiful.

So engrossed in their conversation were they that they did not notice the elegantly dressed man in the pearl-grey riding habit astride the black stallion who came cantering up behind them. He, however, had ample opportunity to observe them.

That hair! I would recognize it anywhere. Like a goddess in a Titian painting, thought Aristide. At last I have found her without her aunt.

Aristide rode past them and then turned his horse sharply in front of them. He bowed.

"Bonjour, mesdemoiselles. *A votre service*," he greeted pleasantly, removing his broad-brimmed hat.

Daphne nodded at him and attempted to continue walking, but Aristide dismounted and walked along beside them, leading his horse. A desultory conversation began as Daphne introduced Nana. It seemed they were already acquainted.

Aristide and Nana spoke rapidly to one another in French, laughing and making a great many jokes that Daphne did not understand. Nana was flirting with Aristide outrageously, playing the coquette as though she were on stage. It was quite a performance. Daphne was annoyed with both of them and felt excluded.

Soon Aristide said that he had to be going and, leaning toward Daphne spoke to her in English. He knew that Nana did not know English.

"Why did you send back my flowers?"

"I can't receive gifts from gentlemen," Daphne replied primly. "My aunt won't allow it."

"I hope we'll see one another again soon. I live only for you." With that last extraordinary remark, uttered in a warm, caressing voice, he mounted his stallion and cantered away.

"What a foolish man!" exclaimed Daphne to Nana when he was gone.

"I don't think so, *chérie*. He is all that a man should be—elegant, graceful and rich. But I don't know why I waste my time flirting with him. Celine

216

has him in her trap. That evil woman," she said, her face puckered with disdain.

From that morning on, Aristide joined them each day, as they walked in the park. There was something mesmerizing about the man. Daphne wanted to see him, but always after she had seen him, she felt slightly soiled. Once or twice she and Nana varied their walks to avoid him, but he found them. There was something inevitable about his presence, something destined.

Every afternoon Daphne wrote long letters to Rene, reviewed her few tender memories, and sighed. Somehow, no matter how hard she tried, Rene seemed to be slipping further and further away from her.

The Moulin de la Galette was an open-air pleasure garden on the outskirts of Paris, near Montmartre. Every night in the warm months of the year, Parisians gathered at the Moulin to walk beneath the trees in the light of Japanese lanterns, listening to the music of dance bands. At times there was dancing, lively polkas and waltzes that left the dancers pink-cheeked and breathless. Pretty girls performed every night, doing splits and the famed cancan. The Moulin also was open on Saturdays and Sundays during the day and was crowded with people from every layer of Paris society—laborers, shopgirls and countesses.

Daphne had never been to the Moulin, and Nana offered to go with her one Sunday afternoon. Daphne wore a simple blue and white cotton dress, for although it was October, the day was warm. The dress had a tight striped bodice over a white blouse, and a large bustle of the same striped material made up the overskirt. Beneath that was a white, lace-trimmed petticoat. It was a country dress, rather like the ones milkmaids wore, and Daphne was very pleased with the way she looked.

Daphne and Nana strolled arm in arm through the crowds, sharing a bag of caramelized peanuts. In the center of the park was the windmill that gave the pavilion its name, turning lazily in the gentle breeze. Daphne's blue eyes were wide as she studied the many people, marveled over the pretty flowers and shrubs growing between the paths, and listened to the music floating in the air.

"Oh, Nana, it's so lovely here. It's as though we were characters in a play."

"I think you wish you were an actress, Daphne. I must be careful or you will try to creep into my profession and steal my laurels," Nana laughed.

"Well, I do daydream sometimes about being a great actress. Standing on the stage saying wonderful lines wearing a beautiful gown, all those people looking at me, and then the applause!" Daphne grew starry-eyed.

"A beautiful picture, but very little like the real thing. You are usually frightened, and it's too hot because of all the lights, and you are angry at someone else in the cast, and the dressmaker has made your dress so tight you can't breathe, and all the while you wonder how those fools in the audience don't notice these things. For a moment, you are caught up in what you are saying, and then you realize that your shoes are too tight or that the actor who is playing your lover has eaten garlic for lunch and you have to kiss him again in the second act!"

Daphne and Nana dissolved into giggles at the thought of the garlic-scented lover.

"Oh, Nana, you just say those things to be funny. It can't really be like that. It must be marvelous. As though you were living in a dream."

"The only problem is that it's someone else's dream, not mine," answered Nana. "But one does not come to the Moulin to talk philosophy. One comes to laugh and to meet one's lovers and to dance and to eat ice cream. I am ravenous."

They both wanted an ice, and so a few minutes later they were seated at a small wrought iron table, where they could see the dancers whirling a few feet away.

"How fortunate for me to find you amid this crowd. I am indeed a lucky man," boomed a deep male voice.

Daphne looked up, startled by Aristide's sudden appearance. She blushed slightly under his mocking gaze and stammered a greeting.

"May I join you ladies?" Nana motioned to him to sit down and called the waiter so that Aristide could order a drink.

Aristide set about making himself agreeable to Daphne, telling her stories about his two years in the American West. He was a born storyteller and soon Nana and Daphne were both caught up in his narration. His story was so vivid that Daphne nearly felt the baking summer sun and the icy cold blizzards of the Rocky Mountains. She could almost smell the cattle on the trail, taste the clear mountain spring water, and see the Indians riding their fast appaloosas across the range.

"Jesse James wasn't such a bad man. He was quite good to his mother, for instance."

"You've met Jesse James," breathed Daphne.

"Many times. Jesse and I were good friends, that is if a wanted man can have friends. We had some good times together in Mexico. He used to call me Frenchie. Well, I could tell you more of my adventures, but perhaps those stories are not fit for ladies. They are a bit wild."

Daphne wondered what those stories were. How exciting it must be to live in the West. Why, Jesse James was an infamous killer and here was someone who had been his friend.

Soon Daphne, Nana and Aristide left their pleasant table beneath an arbor and mingled with the crowd. It was now the middle of the afternoon and the Moulin was jammed. The sun was at its hottest.

Daphne passed a hand over her brow. She was perspiring from the heat. The crowds pressed against her until the heat became insufferable. She wiped her upper lip with her handkerchief. She was becoming unsteady on her feet and she felt dizzy. Very slowly the world began to spin around, its colors making a kaleidoscope before her eyes. Daphne was about to tell Nana that she felt ill when she suddenly fell forward in a faint.

Aristide lifted her up while Nana chafed her hands and applied the smelling salts she always carried with her. Daphne came around suddenly.

"Come, we better go home," said Nana. "Will you carry her to my carriage, Aristide? It is just outside the main gate."

Aristide gripped Daphne firmly in his arms. She struggled slightly, but was too weak to walk. Aristide placed her gently in Nana's carriage and then, after making sure that there was nothing more to be done, watched the carriage drive off.

"Odd that such a young, healthy looking girl should faint. Most unusual," he mused.

Nana had much the same feeling about the incident, but she had a suspicion of the cause of Daphne's sudden malady. It had seemed to her for some time that Daphne often looked pale on their morning walks together. She determined to have Daphne examined by her own physician, who would surely be able to confirm or deny her suspicions. Nana looked with pity at Daphne, for she was sure that the girl was too innocent to know what was happening within her own body.

"I don't see why you had to call the doctor," protested Daphne once she was comfortably ensconced in Nana's apartment. "I feel much better. I'm not at all sick. It was just all the people and the heat."

Nana shushed her. "Certainly, *ma petite*, but it is well to see the doctor anyway. I think you do not feel very well these days. Now sit back quietly and sip your tea," advised Nana.

Daphne looked around her with interest, for she had never been in Nana's bedroom before. It was a large, dimly lit chamber, most of which was taken up by an enormous bed with an elaborate gilt headboard decorated with Cupids and garlands of flowers. In one corner stood Nana's walnut dressing table. It had a sprigged muslin skirt. The floor in front of it was scattered with talcum powder and the table was covered with a litter of toilet articles, flowers, hairpins and little keepsakes. Next to it was a Japanese screen with a picture of herons flying across a peaceful sky, behind which was a washstand. The room was so like Nana herself, expansive, a bit untidy, but beautiful and warm. Daphne sank back against the chaise, and closed her eyes. Despite her protests that she didn't need a doctor, she was beginning to worry about her health.

Soon, Doctor Fournier bustled into the room. The doctor was a thin, stooping man with thinning grey hair, a small, sharply pointed grey beard and pince-nez that seemed to be in constant danger of falling down his nose. He examined Daphne briefly and asked her questions.

"Is the fainting dangerous, Doctor?"

"Not at all, my dear. In your condition, it is perfectly normal."

"My condition?" repeated Daphne, alarmed.

"Why, yes, don't you know? You are with child."

Daphne's mouth went dry. A thousand feelings fought within her. The idea that she and Rene might have a child had never occurred to her, for she had grown up in complete ignorance of such things. When she was able to speak again, the doctor had gone and Nana was by her side, holding her hand.

"It is a great shock, no?" Nana asked.

"Why, yes," Daphne stammered. "I can't believe it. I never thought . . ."

Nana laughed despite herself. "But, Daphne, the child came of your love for your Rene, of the two of you being close together. That is that. You are pregnant."

"I can hardly believe it. Why, I'm going to have a baby!" exclaimed Daphne. "Rene and I! Oh, he will be so happy. Oh, Nana! How wonderful, a baby!"

Daphne's face glowed with happiness. "And to think I was so stupid I didn't even realize. I must talk to someone who's done this before and find out all about it. Do you know anyone, Nana?"

"Yes," she answered softly. "I."

"But . . . ." said Daphne, wanting to ask what had happened, but too afraid that the question would be too painful for Nana.

"Ah, he is fine. My Louis is five and he lives in the country." Nana glowed with a mother's pride as she talked about the boy, rushing to her bedside table to fetch his picture. Louis was a chubby blond boy in a sailor suit, with the same robust good looks as his mother.

"But why don't you keep him with you?" asked Daphne.

"Paris is no place for a child to grow up. Louis is much happier in the country, living on a farm, eating good food and breathing clean air."

"What was it like, having a baby?" asked Daphne. All that afternoon, Daphne and Nana talked and Daphne learned what would be happening to her body in the subsequent months and how the child would be born into the world. It was all incredible to her, but at the same time it filled her with joy. Yet, it was the first time she had heard about most of it.

"You'll have no trouble, Daphne. You are built for children. Now we must get you home or Isabel will worry."

"Do you think she'll be very angry?" asked Daphne.

"No, no. She is a *femme du monde* and she loves you, so she'll be as glad for you as I am. It will come right. You will find your Rene again and the two of you and your child will be happy."

Daphne arrived home looking radiant.

"You look so happy," exclaimed Isabel, wiping her paint-stained hands on her apron, for Daphne had interrupted her at work in her studio.

"Oh, I am," cried Daphne, hugging her aunt, heedless of the oil paints staining her dress.

"What's happened?"

"I'm going to have a baby." Not waiting for Isabel's reaction, Daphne continued, "You're not angry, are you, Aunt Isabel? I want you to be happy for me and for Rene. Isn't it the most wonderful thing?"

Isabel returned Daphne's embrace warmly. She did not think it was entirely wonderful, but she did not want to spoil Daphne's happiness. Isabel was afraid that, in the months to come, Daphne would not find much cause for happiness. Rene was far away, possibly in jail, and Jeb would be furious when he learned of the baby. No, Daphne would certainly not have much to be happy about in the long months of her pregnancy.

"I hope it will make you happy, Daphne, and I'll do anything I can to help you."

"Oh, Aunt Isabel, I love you. You're so wonderful to me. Thank you," cried Daphne, hugging her aunt more tightly. "Oh, Rene will be so happy when he finds out. Surely Papa won't keep us apart now. I know he'll be angry with me, but he can't refuse to let me marry Rene. Think of the scandal!"

Daphne went off to write to her father leaving Isabel deep in thought. She was not as confident of a favorable resolution to all this as Daphne was, but she decided to keep up a cheerful front for her niece's sake.

Aristide called at Isabel's apartment the next morning to find out how Daphne was.

"I am very well, thank you," she smiled up at him. "You see, it was perfectly normal that I fainted, because Rene and I are to have a baby." Daphne beamed at Aristide. "Aren't you glad?"

"Naturally, I must feel your happiness as my own," said Aristide stiffly, for he was deeply shocked by what Daphne had told him and the carefree manner in which she had related this delicate news.

"Good, because I want everyone to be as happy as I am. It makes me feel so much closer to Rene. Oh, no one knows how much I have missed him. But now that will change. Papa will have to help him get out of jail so that we can be married."

Aristide smiled at her skeptically. How extraordinarily naive the girl was!

"I am relieved to find you well, Daphne. If there is anything I can do for you, please tell me."

"Oh, no, but thank you. I have everything now. I am only waiting for Rene and I think he may arrive soon. Good-bye, and thank you so much for calling on me to see how I was feeling."

Chapter 18

Lilleth pulled her cloak more closely around her and shivered as she sat waiting on the hard bench in the cold room. She wondered, if conditions were like this for visitors, what were they like for those inside?

The warder, a hard-looking man with several days' growth of beard, appeared in the doorway, stared at Lilleth insolently and then motioned her to follow him.

They walked down long stone corridors, iron-gates clanking shut behind them, each step taking them farther from the outside world. Lilleth shivered again, but not with cold.

"You can have ten minutes with him," grunted the warder.

Lilleth nodded and entered the room as the warder pulled the door shut behind her. She heard the key grate in the lock. Now she, too, was a prisoner.

Rene stood on the other side of the room. He had

become dreadfully thin and his face was hollow, pinched and terribly sad. He smiled at Lilleth, but did not move toward her. For a few minutes they looked at one another and did not speak.

"Rene," Lilleth suddenly cried, crossing the room and taking him in her arms.

"Lilleth, I . . ." He was interrupted by a violent fit of coughing that racked his thin frame. "I'm glad you came. It's like a breath of air."

"That cough is serious," remarked Lilleth, much concerned, but Rene dismissed it with a wave of his hand. "We haven't much time, so I must tell you quickly some important things.

"After the rioting, I became ill and I had to spend months at my mother's, recovering. When I returned to the settlement house last week, I found some letters from Daphne waiting for me. Some were addressed to you in care of me." Lilleth handed him a small packet of letters. Rene's thin fingers touched them reverently and then, in a quick motion, he tucked the letters deep into his shirt. His face had begun to look softer.

"Daphne wrote to me that she is well and in Paris. Her father and aunt sent her there against her will. She is living with an aunt and wants to know how you are. She plans to get away somehow to find you."

Rene shook his head sadly. "There's no point. I may be in here for the full twenty-year sentence. No, no, tell her to forget about me. Oh, Lilleth, it's hard to believe she really loves me, in spite of all we've been through." Rene's voice choked with emotion. "You must tell her to forget me. She'll waste her life waiting for me if she doesn't. Tell her."

"Read the letters first and then we'll talk again," Lilleth advised.

"Lilleth, they won't let me send letters here, so you must write and tell her. Please, Lilleth," begged Rene, "she must not wait for a man who's in jail for twenty years."

"Time's up, lady," said the warder, taking Lilleth roughly by the arm and leading her out of the room. Rene was once more seized by a fit of coughing. Doubling over with pain, he spat blood into a handkerchief. The door behind him opened and another guard took him back to his cell.

The tinkle of crystal and cutlery, and the music of a string quartet made pleasant accompaniments to the lavish dinner. Jeb, Elspeth and Caleb were enjoying an elaborate meal in Pittsburgh's finest restaurant, celebrating the new partnership between Caleb and Jeb. Caleb had finally agreed to purchase some of Jeb's "worthless" iron fields from him, thus relieving some of Jeb's financial problems.

Jeb's face was already becoming rather florid from the wine. Elspeth looked at his glass with disapproval, noting each sip he took. Her glass remained untouched, her face pale and composed, as always. Her ramrod back did not touch the chair. Everything about Elspeth was under complete control, despite the fact that only that morning she had received the most shocking news of recent years.

Daphne was ruined, ruined even more completely than even Elspeth in one of her blackest moods could have predicted. Elspeth allowed her mind to wander as she considered Daphne's letter and her condition. Her hand toyed idly with her spoon and she gazed off into space. She, for one, wished to wash her hands of the girl and to write her off as a bad business, just as she had once done with Isabel so many years ago. Elspeth's face grew even tighter as she thought of her sister.

I was right to turn away from Isabel, she thought. She was on the path to sin. Elspeth pursed her lips and took a deep breath.

Caleb's voice brought her back from her memories. "Elspeth, you're a million miles away. I was telling Jeb that I want to make a toast."

"Yes, it's a night for toasts. We're here to celebrate," she answered with a strained smile.

"To my bride-to-be, Daphne."

Caleb raised his glass and looked expectantly from Jeb to Elspeth. They were both staring at him, and neither had raised their glasses for the toast. Then Elspeth broke the spell by picking up her glass and raising it high. With a piercing look at Jeb, she said harshly, "To Daphne, your bride-to-be."

Jeb lifted his glass, a little hesitantly, and a silence descended upon the group.

"So," said Caleb, wondering at their odd behavior, "when does Daphne come home?"

Jeb looked at Elspeth helplessly, indicating that she must answer. She had always been quicker than he.

"Not for several months. Winter is not the best time to make an Atlantic crossing. In fact, we received a letter from her just today. She begged to be allowed to stay until next summer. Of course, Jeb and I can deny her nothing. Such a sweet, innocent girl, so unspoiled."

Caleb broke in, "I think that I may take a trip to

Europe this summer. Daphne and I could be married in Paris and then make a short tour of Europe. I have not been to Europe since just after I graduated from Yale.

"You know, Jeb, while I'm there, I think I'll make a detour to England and examine that Bessemer process everyone is so excited about. I'm sure we can find ways to really cut costs by studying the English methods. Caleb laughed. He was in high spirits, for he had just completed his highly advantageous purchase of Jeb's mines and Daphne at last seemed ready to marry him.

"Yes," said Caleb, "I think 1878 is going to be a very good year for us all."

Elspeth nodded vigorously, vowing to herself that she'd see to it that Daphne would do her duty to her family and marry Caleb. She thought of how Daphne had deceived her and spurned her good advice. Elspeth's face was so grim that even Jeb wondered what she was thinking.

The grey stone walls of Rene's cell were so damp that moisture ran down them. None of the sounds of the outside world ever reached the cell. The only noises were the endless dripping of slimy water from the walls, the scurrying of rats, and the footsteps of the guards as they made their rounds. Rene rubbed his hands together for warmth and put one of them under his arm to warm it. The other hand held Daphne's letter.

Tears ran down his cheeks as he paced to and fro in his cell, reading her letters over and over again.

Dear Rene, I miss you constantly and think

of you every day, every moment. There are
brief times when I am happy, but I hate myself then, for I am afraid that you are suffering. My only comfort is the memory of the
times we spent together and the knowledge
that we will be together again someday. I
can wait forever, Rene. I love you with all
my heart.

Daphne's words made Rene feel close to her once
again and he kissed the letter, brushing the paper
gently against his face.

How can I give her up? he asked himself. She is
everything to me, my only hope in this wasteland.
And she says she loves me, she is so willing to wait.

A voice inside him warned him that it would be
wrong of him to ask her to wait, or even to allow it.
She might be a middle-aged woman by the time he
was free and she would hate him for taking her
youth.

You may not have a choice, his voice warned
him. You did beg Lilleth to write her and say she was
not to wait for you. Had Lilleth done so? Rene had
no way of reaching her. He would have to wait until
she visited again, whenever that might be. Only then
would he know whether Lilleth had written to
Daphne and told her that their love was over forever.
Waiting to see Lilleth would be a continuing torment
and he prayed silently that she would come again
soon.

Rene continued reading through the pile of letters, savoring each one as he read it. Rene finally
opened the last letter. He had been reading them in
the order in which Daphne had written them. His

hands trembled as he unfolded it, sad that he had reached the last one.

I probably will never get another letter from her, he thought. Not after Lilleth tells her what I have told her to. A terrible pain went through his heart.

Rene read the letter slowly, and then, as he realized what it said, he read faster, trying to understand just what Daphne was telling him.

Stunned, he sat down on his cot and put his head in his hands, staring at the stone floor for a long, long time.

"What have I done," he moaned. "What have I done to her? Oh, God, what will she think when Lilleth tells her that it's over between us? I must find some way to stop her."

Rene's mind raced frantically, searching for a way to prevent Lilleth from writing the letter to Daphne. There was no way. He was a prisoner and was not allowed to send messages to the outside world. He would just have to wait until Lilleth came to see him again and by then the damage would have been done.

"I can't wait twenty years to see my child," he said aloud. "I *won't* wait."

Suddenly Rene leapt up from his bunk and began to walk slowly around the room, examining the walls. With his fingernails, he began to pick painstakingly at the mortar.

Daphne sat before the fire in Isabel's cozy parlor. It was a cold, rainy day in late November. Bare tree branches brushed against the windows. Daphne sighed, wondering if the weather brightened at all. But no, the sky was still a leaden grey.

For some reason Daphne felt restless. She wished she could go out and visit someone. She longed for someone to talk to, but there was no one. Isabel was locked in her studio painting and had given instructions that she should not be disturbed. Daphne sighed again.

Daphne picked up the book, *Wuthering Heights*, and began to read, but in a few seconds she put the book aside, unable to concentrate. She had her own tragedy now, and this one she was reading didn't seem romantic anymore. It was painful. I'll think of something more cheerful, she decided. Of when the baby and Rene and I are together again.

Daphne furrowed her brow and settled more comfortably in the overstuffed chair. What shall we name the baby, she asked herself. But this was too easy, for she had thought of it so many times that the decision was made. Miranda for a girl and Laurence for a boy. She tried to imagine living in a small cottage with Rene and the baby, but she could not make the picture materialize.

"Oh, Rene, Rene, why don't you write to me? Why hasn't Lilleth written? I can't stand not knowing." Daphne wrung her hands. Burying her head in her arms, she began to weep.

The maid found her that way when she brought in the mail.

"Cheer up, my dear. The mail may have some glad news for you," she said.

"Oh, Annette, I hope so. I have so little hope left. It's been so long since I've seen him."

Annette nodded sympathetically and, giving the letters to Daphne, left the room.

Daphne examined the two envelopes addressed

to her. The first was from her father and, opening it hurriedly, she set the second letter aside.

Dear Daphne,

We are shocked and dismayed to learn of your condition. We are most especially appalled by the proud way in which you reported it to us. A woman in your situation cannot possibly feel anything other than the deepest shame.

It is out of the question for you to have anything further to do with the man who is responsible for what has happened to you. We will do everything in our power to stop you from seeing him.

Luckily, your aunt and I are charitable people and we are willing to take you back when all this is over. You are indeed fortunate to have such understanding relations and we hope that you will realize this and be grateful.

Of course you may not keep the child. You will place it with a family of its own station in life and they will raise it as their own.

Something may perhaps be salvaged from the wreck you have made of your life. Caleb is still willing to marry you. He knows nothing of your condition and you may be sure that your aunt and I will keep your shameful secret.

I hope that this letter finds you chastised.

Father

Daphne crumpled the letter savagely and threw it to the floor. Already tears were streaming down her face.

"How can they be so cruel!" she cried.

Looking at the other letter on the tray, Daphne felt a sudden surge of hope that it might be from Lilleth. Picking it up with trembling hands, still shaken by the meanness of her father's letter, she examined the envelope. It was from Lilleth! It read:

Dear Daphne,

    I saw Rene in prison and gave him your letters. He is serving a twenty-year sentence, but is as well as can be expected. He asks me to tell you that he considers everything to be finished between the two of you. You must understand that there is nothing Rene can do for you while he is in jail. My dear, you would be better off forgetting him.

The words swam in front of her eyes. She tossed this letter aside, too stunned to comprehend why Lilleth had been so harsh.

Chapter 19

Some time later, Isabel found Daphne slumped in her chair, deathly pale. She picked up the letter and began to read it, an expression of deep concern on her face.

"Have you read the whole letter?" she asked when she had finished. Daphne shook her head. "I think you should, for it explains a great deal."

Daphne took up the sheet once again with a trembling hand and with a frightened heart she began to read.

> Rene feels that it would be selfish on his part to bind you to him when he will be a prisoner for the next twenty years. He is afraid that you will feel you have thrown away your youth on him. I believe that love is what prompts him to give you up. I know that Rene would not wish me to have told you this, but I believe that any decision

about your future together should not be made by Rene alone. You have a right to know all the facts and as a friend to you both, I am conveying them to the best of my ability.

Daphne breathed a sigh of relief and began to smile through her tears. "When he told Lilleth to write to me, he couldn't have read my letter yet. He mustn't have known about the baby!" cried Daphne. "But he must have that letter by now."

Isabel hugged Daphne to her. "Oh, Aunt Isabel, I know Rene will find a way out of that prison. I can feel it. And the baby will be such a comfort to me until we can be together again." Daphne put her hands to her abdomen and was still for a moment. Strength was beginning to return.

The streets of Paris began to smell of pine needles as huge Christmas trees were brought in from the countryside. Daphne walked quickly through the streets, wrinkling her nose in pleasure from all the lovely Christmas smells. Around her were crowds of people on their way home from work, many of them carrying boxes and packages full of Christmas presents. Everyone was talking at once and all the street vendors were crying out in demanding voices.

Suddenly hungry, Daphne stopped at a chestnut vendor's stall and bought a handful of the piping hot nuts. Daphne walked slowly along the street, letting herself be carried along by the crowd as she ate the steaming hot, fragrant chestnuts.

"Ah, I am pleased to see that your appetite is as good as ever," said a voice behind her.

Daphne spun around. "Aristide," she cried, smiling at him and holding out her free hand, which was still warm from holding the chestnuts.

He was surprised at the warmth of her greeting. He thought they had parted on cool terms. Daphne looked more beautiful than ever. Her cheeks were full and rosy and her eyes sparkled. She exuded happiness and well being though he did not see how this could be. She was, after all, pregnant without being married.

"My, it's good to see you, Daphne. You look wonderful," he said, not letting go of her hand. "We're very close to Tortoni's. Do you have time to have a drink with me?" Daphne agreed readily and the two of them walked to the well-known café, arm in arm.

When Daphne removed her overcoat, Aristide saw that she had thickened about the waist. He looked admiringly at her, for she now had a womanly glow about her and an air of self-assurance that she had been lacking when they first met.

"And how do you like Paris?"

"Oh, I love it. I feel so at home here now. And I have so many friends. We are planning a wonderful Christmas. Nana's son Louis is coming from Nantes to join us. Aunt Isabel and I are very excited and, of course, Nana is in heaven."

Daphne stopped to bite into the chocolate éclair the waiter had put in front of her. It was delicious. The custard oozed between her fingers and she licked them like a child. Aristide found the gesture both touching and erotic.

"It seems ever so long since we were on the ship together. I feel as though I'm a different person. I've heard from Rene at last, too. Just today, in fact. He's delighted about the baby. And he's agreed that Miranda and Laurence are the best names. But I'm boring you."

"Nonsense. You could never bore me. Just hearing your voice and looking at you is enough to fascinate me."

"Ah, Aristide, you are so charming. But I do believe you're trying to turn my head. You must remember that I am an old hag of eighteen and *enceinte* as well." Daphne giggled and took a sip of her sweet, milky coffee.

"And I believe that you are flirting with me," Aristide answered, laughing.

They talked easily together until Daphne said, "Well, I must run." She pulled on her gloves and adjusted her fur-trimmed blue bonnet. "There's always so much to do just before Christmas and we want Louis to really enjoy himself. *Joyeux Noël*," she finished merrily, allowing Aristide to help her with her coat. He relished the momentary closeness. Daphne had changed from being merely a very pretty girl to being an exciting woman.

Daphne's plans for Christmas went perfectly. Louis was charmed by all the surprises and pronounced everything *"fantastique."* Daphne in turn was charmed by Louis, an angelic-looking boy of five with blond ringlets falling to his shoulders. In his navy blue velvet suit with its knickers, lace cuffs and collar, he was the picture of innocence. Nana was terribly proud of him and adored him, although she tried to hide it behind a gruff manner. She deceived no one.

The *bûche de Noël* was a particular triumph. The

little boy's eyes lit up when the long cake, frosted to resemble a log, was brought into the room.

"Mama, what a lovely cake," he cried.

"Silly boy, that's not a cake, that's a stick that we're going to beat you with if you're not good."

Louis feigned horror. "But I am always good, Mama. Isn't that so, Aunt Daphne. You won't let Mama hit me."

"Why, you are as good an actor as your mother," interjected Isabel. "Please, Daphne, let's settle this argument. Why don't you cut the log!"

Daphne did so and Louis immediately began to tease his mother, saying that she must be very silly if she didn't know the difference between a log and a cake.

After dinner they all settled in the small parlor. Louis played with his toys on the hearth rug while Daphne, Isabel and Nana sat in a half-circle around him, watching him fondly and gazing contentedly into the fire.

"I wonder where Rene and I will go when we can be together again," mused Daphne. "He wanted to go West. Think how exciting that would be! Cowboys and gold rushes and rampaging buffalos and Indians. Why Miranda or Laurence will practically grow up on horseback!"

"But it's so far from Paris," Nana objected. "We will miss you."

"You can do a tour of the American West. I'm sure you'd be a great success in America. And Aunt Isabel could come with you and visit. I'm sure there must be lots of wonderful things out there to paint."

But suddenly she stopped, realizing that Nana

was looking at Louis with an expression of deep concern. "Louis," she said sharply, "you are sitting too close to the fire and it is giving you a rash."

"Oh, you mean the little patches, Mama? They're nothing. I have lots on my tummy, too." The child went back to his play, unconcerned. Nana hurried to him and knelt beside him on the floor, peeling his clothes away. She cried out when she saw that his stomach was indeed covered with a rash.

"Silly Mama," chided Louis. "They don't even hurt."

Nana put her hand to Louis' forehead and frowned deeply.

"What is it?" asked Daphne.

"I don't know," answered Nana. "Call the doctor while I put him to bed."

Nana took Louis off to bed, ignoring his howls of protest. Daphne rang for the maid to get the doctor and then she and Isabel waited nervously for his arrival.

The diagnosis was scarlet fever and the whole house was quarantined. Daphne was not allowed to nurse the boy, for it was feared that she might catch the disease from him, and in her condition that might be fatal. Isabel worried that the baby might have been affected.

A few days later, Daphne awakened with a rash on her chest and a high fever. Ignoring her own health, Isabel insisted on nursing Daphne. Daphne seemed well enough at first, but as the hours dragged by and her fever rose higher and higher, she became delirious.

"Rene!" she cried again and again, holding out her arms. Each time Isabel would rush up to her and ease her back onto her pillow.

That evening, Dr. Fournier came to examine her again, and afterward he gestured to Isabel to follow him out of the room. "Her condition is very serious. I've rarely seen the disease take hold so fast," he said wearily. "We'll try applying ice packs to the body to see if that will break the fever. It will be painful for Daphne, I am afraid, and she'll resist, but you must do it if we are to save her."

Isabel nodded. She was already exhausted from nursing Louis, who had been ill for many days. His fever still had not broken.

"If we can break her fever tonight, there is still hope for Daphne and for the baby."

All that night, Isabel and Annette struggled with Daphne to keep her wrapped in the ice packs. In her delirium she thought that they were Jeb and Caleb. Daphne fought against them with all her strength, shouting at them. Eventually she wore herself out and fell into a fitful sleep.

Daphne awoke with a start, screaming: the dream's last image still hung before her eyes. Rene was hanging from a gallows, dead. Daphne screamed again and fell back in a faint.

Revived by her sleep, Daphne began to struggle once again with Isabel and Annette. Finally, they tied her to the bed and left her struggling vainly at her bonds.

"I can't stand seeing her like this," said Isabel, exhausted and overwrought.

In the morning, the doctor came again. He

looked at Daphne sadly. "The ice packs have failed," he said, shaking his head. "Her fever has not broken."

"What hope is there?" asked Isabel.

"We must all pray. She is in God's hands now," the doctor said as gently as he could. When he returned the following day, Daphne was worse.

Dr. Fournier examined Daphne and then turned to Isabel. "I am afraid she has gone into labor."

Isabel clapped her hand to her mouth in horro "But she is not even conscious and the baby is not due for four months yet!"

The doctor nodded gravely. "I believe that the high fever has damaged the child and the body now seeks to expel it. It is probably for the best. I will stay with her all day. It will be a most difficult business. It would be best if you waited outside. I will call a midwife to assist me."

Isabel agreed and went to sit in her room to wait. Throughout the long day, she heard Daphne moaning on occasion and sometimes babbling. Isabel put her hands to her ears to try to block out the sounds. In the months since Daphne had come to live with her, Isabel had come to love her niece as though she were her daughter. She hated to think what the loss of the child would do to Daphne . . . if she even lived to know of it.

Late that night, and without ever coming to herself, Daphne was delivered of a girl. The child was dead. Later Daphne fell into a deep sleep, almost a coma. Her fever still raged. She remained in that state for three days and Nana came to nurse her. "My son is recovering in the country. Daphne is my friend and I want to be with her when she wakes up."

And Nana was with Daphne when, on the fourth day, she stirred and spoke clearly. It was Nana who told Daphne what had happened to her. The two hugged one another, their tears mingling, sobbing for the baby.

"I wish I were dead as well," moaned Daphne, turning her face to the wall.

"You mustn't. You have much to live for. You are young and you will have other children. Think of Rene."

"I may never see Rene again. It will be twenty years before he is released and we will both be old by then. He may die while he is in prison. I dream of it all the time and the dreams are terrible."

Nana held Daphne as she cried. After that day, Daphne did not cry again. At least, not while anyone was with her. But she did not recover her strength. She remained in bed, too weak to get up and too demoralized to fight.

The winter ended and the first signs of spring showed themselves in Paris, but still Daphne did not get well. Lassitude had taken her over entirely.

One morning Isabel burst into Daphne's room and pulled open the thick curtains to reveal a fresh spring day. "A letter has come for you. It's from America and I think it's from your friend Lilleth."

For the first time in many weeks, Daphne sat up eagerly. She took the letter and opened it, reading it anxiously. Isabel watched her, saddened by the change Daphne's illness had made in her. She was very thin, with great hollows in her cheeks and dark circles under her blue eyes. Gone was the womanly bloom of pregnancy. Daphne now had the body of a child. But something changed in Daphne as she read the letter.

"Rene has escaped," she whispered to her aunt. "He's *escaped*. Rene has escaped!" She cried, joy suffusing her thin, pale face.

Chapter 20

Caleb stood in the center of the room, holding his black beaver hat in his hands, not quite knowing what to do with himself. He looked around, scrutinizing the room, trying to discover what kind of person its owner was. It was a strange, exotic, colorful room, hardly the sort of setting in which one would expect to find an American spinster.

At any moment Daphne would enter the room. Caleb smiled. Jeb had explained that Daphne was now anxious to marry him. While Caleb suspected Jeb of overstating the case, he was sure that the girl would be only too happy to escape the dull life she was living with her spinster aunt and go with him on a glamorous honeymoon in Italy.

His imagination conjured up a picture of his Daphne, beautiful and young, with that supple body that begged to be caressed. She was difficult, but it would be worth his effort to make her his. Despite her childishness, there was something tough and determined about her that made Caleb want to protect her and break her at the same time. She was like a fine mare, fiery and spirited, but she needed breaking.

Lucky that aunt of hers isn't at home, thought Caleb. If she's anything like Elspeth, she'll watch us every minute. No, it's better if I see Daphne alone. I have a great deal of persuading to do. Caleb smiled. Yes, Daphne needs a real man.

Caleb tapped his fingers impatiently on a lacquered china tea chest. Where was that girl? It seemed as though the maid had been gone for hours. Caleb was not used to waiting.

Quick footsteps sounded, running down the hall. The double doors of the parlor flew open and Daphne rushed in. She was still thin and pale, her eyes shining almost feverishly, her hair loose and tumbling over her shoulders. She wore a white nightgown that trailed the floor, covering her bare feet. At the sight of Caleb, she stopped short and stood still, staring.

"Caleb," she whispered.

"You've been ill," he said, shocked by her appearance.

Daphne nodded. Approaching a sofa like a sleepwalker, she sat down slowly. "I thought you might be ... someone else."

Caleb was puzzled, who else could she have expected? He had told the maid he was Daphne's fiancé from America. Could Daphne have another suitor?

"What do you mean?" he asked sharply.

"Rene. I thought you were Rene."

"Daphne, what are you talking about? I have come to take you away. We'll get married immediately and then leave for Italy. You'll soon be well again. Call your maid, have her dress you and we'll go right now." Caleb spoke as though he were instructing a child. Her father had mentioned that she had had scarlet fever, but Caleb had not expected its effects to be so severe. She didn't seem herself. But then Daphne seemed to snap out of the shock that had come over her when she saw Caleb.

"I'll do nothing of the sort, Caleb," she said with spirit. "I have no intention of marrying you today. tomorrow or ever, for that matter. I am perfectly well, merely surprised to see you." Daphne glared at Caleb defiantly, waiting to see what his reaction would be.

"So far, I've overlooked your stubbornness in refusing to marry me, but the time for that is past. I have come all the way to Paris to marry you and marry you I will. Now go get dressed, or I'll dress you myself."

"You'll do no such thing. You can't marry me against my will. I consider myself married to another. As you surely must know, I have never loved you and have never wanted to marry you. This is all your and my father's doing. Now please go."

"Why, you would order me out just like that?" Caleb was furious. The journey had been tiring and he had buoyed himself with Jeb's assurance that Daphne was truly ready to marry him. Yet here she was, sounding like the arrogant Daphne he had suffered over before! How dare she?

Struggling to control himself, Caleb sat down in a chair opposite Daphne and busied himself with lighting a cigar. For some moments neither of them spoke as Caleb selected a cigar from his case, cut off the end, sniffed it, and, putting it in his mouth, puffed on it until it was lit. Removing the cigar from between his lips, he exhaled a cloud of blue smoke. "So tell me," he said, "about this Rene of yours. Some French dandy you have met here in Paris?"

Daphne was silent for a moment, quickly considering what to do. Was it better to keep silent? Clearly Jeb had told him nothing. Daphne decided that if he had known about Rene and the baby, Caleb wouldn't be here now. Surely he wouldn't want a woman who had carried another man's child.

"No, Rene is not French. He is an American and well known to you. Rene LeBrun." Daphne watched Caleb's face carefully and was not surprised to see the hatred there. "He is an enemy of yours, I know, but he is my lover. My father sent me here because he knew that Rene and I had been meeting secretly. We planned to run away and get married, but my father kidnapped me during the riots. Rene was sent to jail. You have all conspired to keep us apart, but you will not be able to. We are destined for one another."

Caleb's face turned red with anger and then white with cold fury. He looked at Daphne as though he had never seen her before. She looked so different from the pretty, spoiled girl he had known. Gone was the coyness, and the innocence as well. Daphne looked at him directly and openly. She had changed in more than looks. She was no longer a girl who did not know her own power, but a woman who was sure of herself. Even so, Caleb found the claim of her love for Rene impossible to believe. What did Rene have to offer her?

"Your father told me nothing about this," he stated flatly.

"Of course not," Daphne replied bitterly. "He was trying to sell me to you to save himself. Oh, don't look so surprised, I know all about his business failures. He didn't want you to refuse to buy me. Of course he didn't tell you about Rene."

Caleb had never heard Daphne talk like this. She seemed so worldly, so strong.

"Rene and I were to have had a child. When I was ill with scarlet fever, I lost her. Miranda. Now you know the whole story. Go away, please." Daphne closed her eyes and slumped against the sofa.

Caleb forced himself to smile. He needed time, time to decide what to do. Everything Daphne had said had wounded him deeply, hurt his pride. He needed a chance to find the most fitting punishment for her behavior.

"Of course, now that I understand your position, I will not trouble you further," he said gently. "You are wrong about your father selling you to me. We were both motivated by love of you and that same sincere good feeling causes me always to wish you well, Daphne. I shall be in Paris for a few days. Perhaps I shall call upon you again to see how you are." And with that, Caleb picked up his hat and left.

Daphne sighed with relief. Caleb's gracious departure seemed too good to be true.

Caleb paced up and down his hotel room, oblivious to his ornate surroundings. He was in a world of his own, a world dominated by anger and vengeance.

"No one does this to Caleb Winters! I refuse to allow that girl to get the better of me. I'll show her who's master. And that father of hers . . . I'll deal with him later! Trying to pull the wool over my eyes. Did he really think I'd never find out?"

Caleb raged on and on, inflaming himself still further, Daphne's words ringing in his ears. He continued to puff furiously on his cigar, pacing and thinking, until the taste of it sickened him and he stubbed it out violently.

That girl needs to be taught a lesson, and I'm the man to teach her, Caleb vowed. Says I can't force her to marry me. We'll see about that. A little money in the right hands and we'll be legally married, and then she'll be mine forever to do with as I will. I'll teach her . . . Caleb smiled in satisfaction, and set out to arrange matters.

Caleb wrapped Daphne in the fur lap rug. It was quite a warm day for April, with a hazy blue sky and a slight breeze blowing. Summer was in the air. Even so, Daphne shivered slightly and rubbed her hands together inside the fur muff. It was the first time she had been out of doors since her illness.

I wonder what made me agree to take a drive with Caleb? thought Daphne as the carriage began to roll smoothly away from the curb, pulled by a beautifully matched pair of bays. It was so kind of him to offer, after all that's happened between us. I can afford to be generous, now that I have Rene. Daphne sighed happily. She was hoping to receive a letter from him very soon, telling her where to meet him. Would it be New York? Boston? Daphne forced herself to listen. Caleb had been talking to her.

"Ah, Paris is more beautiful than I remembered. How I envy your living here, Daphne. And this day! It makes me feel wonderful. Great things are in the air."

Daphne looked more closely at Caleb. She rarely had heard him talk so effusively before. But as Caleb went on to talk of ordinary matters, his plans to visit the Louvre and Notre Dame, Daphne let her thoughts drift.

She was beginning to realize how much she had missed the great city when she had been shut up in her sickroom. All around them, Paris bustled. It was a city that conducted its life out of doors. The smell of bakeries and pastry shops tickled her nose. Piles of fresh vegetables and fish on melting blocks of ice stood in front of restaurants as grocers haggled with restaurant chefs. It thrilled Daphne to see the plane trees that lined the streets showing their first green shoots.

She turned to Caleb anxious to share all this with him, but something stopped her. She felt a sudden certainty of danger. Caleb was dangerous and she had been foolish to come out with him. Daphne watched Caleb closely, but his face was now a mask; he revealed nothing.

Soon she found herself in a section of the city that was unfamiliar to her. Caleb had turned the carriage off the broad avenue into a maze of narrow side streets. Caleb pulled the horses to a stop outside a small, ancient church. He handed the reins to a young boy standing outside and told him to wait.

Turning to Daphne, Caleb gave her his most winning smile. "Have you ever been here before?" Daphne shook her head. "Then it's time you saw this church, which is one of the most carefully preserved Romanesque chapels in Paris. It is a little discovery of mine. The carvings are exquisite."

Daphne sensed danger, but could hardly refuse to explore the church. She accepted Caleb's hand and stepped down from the carriage, entering the church on his arm.

Inside it was dark and smelled of incense. It took her a few minutes to adjust to the gloom. There were candles burning at the altar and an old woman prayed silently. The altar was decorated entirely with lilies. It looked as though a funeral had just taken place.

Daphne looked around, trying to see the carvings Caleb had mentioned, wondering why he had brought her into this nearly deserted chapel.

As she looked around, a priest glided onto the altar from a side door. He wore a soiled white vestment and his hair was unkempt, his beard scraggly. The priest motioned them forward. Caleb's grip on Daphne's arm tightened and he led her toward the altar. The old woman rose from her prayers and joined them at the altar, as did a sweeper, who suddenly materialized from the gloom at the back of the church.

When everyone was assembled, Caleb signaled the priest to begin. Daphne and Caleb stood arm in arm before the priest as he spoke to them in Latin. The old woman and the sweeper stood on either side of them.

"What's going on?" hissed Daphne to Caleb.

"We're getting married," he answered with a calm smile of satisfaction on his lips.

"No!" she screamed, her voice echoing throughout the church. "I refuse to marry you. The ceremony can't continue."

"It doesn't matter what you want. I've paid the priest. In another moment we'll be married and you'll be my wife." Caleb gripped her arm savagely.

Daphne's mind raced. Only by running away before the ceremony could be completed could she hope to stay free of Caleb.

The priest motioned to them to kneel, leaning closer to them, his breath reeking of wine. Still holding her arm, Caleb knelt and forced Daphne down. Daphne relaxed completely. Then, with a sudden wrenching movement, she pulled away from him, sending Caleb sprawling on the polished marble steps. Pushing the priest aside, she ran onto the altar and headed for the door at the rear of the altar. The priest, already unsteady on his feet, fell down, blocking Caleb's way for a precious few seconds. Daphne reached the door and slammed it behind her, leaning against it with all her weight. Just as Caleb reached it, she slid the bolt, locking the door.

She searched the small room where the priest changed into his vestments, and found a door. She ran outside, straight into the alley. Caleb would soon realize that she had gone out by the back door and would be doubling around the church to follow her. Her heart beat wildly in her chest as she ran through the winding streets, the sharp paving stones cutting her feet through her soft-soled shoes.

Instinct guided her in her flight. There was no time to think in which direction to run. Daphne knew only that she had to keep running. The streets began to look the same. She did not know where she was. The same passers-by and women hanging out their windows and beating rugs seemed to stare at her in each new street she went down. She began to think that she was running in circles or perhaps not even moving at all. Suddenly she saw what looked like the end of an alley, and she ran toward it, hoping it was one of the main avenues. It was. And as if by magic, there was a hansom cab waiting. Daphne leapt in, exhausted and trembling.

Since Isabel's apartment would not be safe, Daphne gave Nana's address in the Rue Mouffetard and told the driver to hurry. Then she settled back against the cracked leather cushions and tried to catch her breath. She ignored the driver who kept turning around to stare at her, fascinated by the sight of a well-dressed lady, out of breath from running, pale and hauntingly beautiful, her red-blonde hair loosened from its pins and falling down around her shoulders. Daphne strove to quiet herself and coiled up her hair, anchoring it securely with the hairpins she still had.

Nana was in bed drinking her morning chocolate when Daphne arrived. "What is it, *chérie*? I can see from your face that something is wrong," said Nana, patting the bed covers. Daphne sat beside her.

Daphne proceeded to spill out the whole story. Nana listened carefully and said, "He sounds like a ruthless man, and he is obsessed with you. What will you do now?"

"I don't know. I am afraid to go back to Aunt Isabel's for fear that Caleb will find me there and I can't stay here forever."

"It would be unwise for you to stay here too long. He will question the cab drivers and offer rewards until the one who took you here comes forward. That shouldn't take long. He is a rich man and they are poor. You must go away."

"But where?"

"You are still ill, I think. You don't look well yet.

So pale and with that touch of feverish color. I am not sure that you are really well enough to travel."

"I must leave Paris, mustn't I, Nana? Caleb might get the priest and those witnesses to say that I had gone through with the ceremony. If he can convince people that I am his wife, I will never be free of him." Daphne began to weep. "I had thought that I would stay in Paris until Rene told me where to meet him. But I will go back to America and find him. I'm not safe here anymore."

"How will you manage? It's a long way to go unprotected and you still are not well. No, *chérie*, it is too dangerous. I know what it is like to go out on one's own in the world. And what about money? The passage to America is not cheap."

"I have money. I took all my jewels with me from Pittsburgh. I shall manage, Nana—I must."

"But who will accompany you to the ship?" asked Nana.

"Aristide." Nana gaped at her.

"You expect the most sought-after man in Paris to drop everything and help you run off! *Chérie*, it is impossible."

"He will do it for me. When I was last with him, he offered to help me in any way he could."

"But he was only being polite, surely?" Daphne shook her head firmly. "He may help you, but he is not the kind of man who does something for nothing. He will exact his price," muttered Nana darkly.

"I have no choice," answered Daphne, sending Nana's maid running for pen and paper so that she could write to him.

Daphne waited alone in Nana's house for what

seemed to her an eternity. She was in constant fear that Caleb would arrive at any moment. Nana's maid had been instructed to wait at Aristide's house for a reply. Nana was at a pawnbroker's trying to sell Daphne's few jewels: the pearl necklace she had received for her sixteenth birthday, the heavy gold bracelets she had inherited from her mother and the diamond ear bobs she had received from her father for her seventeenth birthday.

At last Nana arrived with the money and the maid with a note from Aristide telling her to be ready at sunset and to disguise herself in men's clothing. Daphne sighed with relief and prepared herself for the coming night's ordeal.

Daphne squeezed Nana's hand and smiled tremulously at her when she heard the bell ring. That would be Aristide.

"Thank you for all you've done for me, Nana. I'll always remember you."

"Come, come, *chérie*. It is not so final. We will meet again in happier times," responded Nana, blinking back her tears. Daphne looked much too frail to undertake such a difficult flight. The men's clothes she wore only served to emphasize her femininity and the delicacy of her frame. "Take care, my child," cried Nana at last, hugging Daphne to her.

"Don't worry. I'm going to join Rene. Nothing can happen to me now." Daphne's face glowed with joy. "I must go now. There is no time to waste."

Downstairs, Aristide waited, roughly dressed in stout leather boots and a heavy cloak that was already glistening with rain.

"Thank you for coming, Aristide," said Daphne

softly, taking his hand in hers and looking into his eyes. "I knew you would. We are friends."

Aristide bowed. "I cannot resist a lady in distress." Especially not such a beautiful one, he added to himself. Daphne looked fragile and lovely. He relished the feel of her body against his as he lifted her onto her horse.

The two rode off in the light rain through the streets of Paris. As they left the city, Daphne turned around for a last look.

I came here as a prisoner, ready to hate Paris, but I have come to love it instead. Only Rene could take me away from you, wonderful city. Perhaps, one day, he and I will come back, Daphne bid farewell to Paris. Then she turned around and concentrated on the road ahead and the long trip to Calais.

After two hours in the saddle, Daphne's body ached and chills racked her thin frame. She had become unused to riding during the long months of her illness, and now each step that the horse took jolted her. The rain had finally stopped, but the wind was still cold.

Daphne and Aristide rode on in silence. They had not spoken since they had left the outskirts of Paris. Daphne was too miserable to speak. It took all her energy just to stay in the saddle. Aristide occupied himself with plans for the future.

I shall install her in a lovely cottage in the country. Somewhere in Provence, I think. We will spend beautiful weeks there together. The country air will do her good and she will fill out again and glow with beauty. Ah, Daphne, it was a lucky day for us both that we met on the Atlantic crossing. And now another stroke of luck—alone together. No one knows where you are. You have only me to look to for help. I could not have planned a better setting for a seduction if I had done it myself. When you are cold and tired, we will stop in a warm inn and have a glass of brandy. The spirits and the heat will awaken your body and then I will take you, Aristide schemed to himself.

Daphne slumped forward against the horse's neck. She jerked herself upright and rubbed her eyes wearily. Would the night never end? It had begun to rain once again, harder this time, and the drops were beginning to soak through Daphne's cloak. She felt that she could go on no longer. Fear of Caleb and desire to be with Rene were replaced by a numbing exhaustion. Daphne wanted only to stop, to rest, to get warm again.

"Aristide!" she cried, but the wind blew the word back in her face. "Aristide!"

Aristide turned around in his saddle. There was something hard and calculating about his face. A cruelty to his mouth that Daphne had never noticed before. His face softened with pity for her. Her lips were almost blue and her cheeks had taken on a chalky pallor.

"I can't go on. Can we stop please, for a few minutes? Surely we have gotten far enough away from Caleb by now," Daphne pleaded.

"Yes, there's an inn not far from here. Another mile. Can you make it?"

Daphne nodded dully and felt the horse plod ahead beneath her. Her hands seemed to be frozen to the reins. In the distance, Daphne could see a light gleaming faintly. She felt a flicker of hope within her breast.

At last they reached the inn and Aristide lifted Daphne from her horse. She weighed so little. Instructions were given for the horses to be fed and watered and Aristide carried Daphne inside.

The innkeeper rushed up to Aristide. Despite his rough clothes, the man recognized him instantly as a member of the gentry. There was something in the dark man's bearing that bespoke authority. Aristide asked for a private room with a fire and the innkeeper led him to a suitable chamber, all the while apologizing for its not being grand enough. The fire was raked up and made to blaze. Aristide ordered brandy and a meal for himself and Daphne.

When the candles had been lit, the innkeeper took a better look at the "boy" the gentleman had carried into the room with him. His suspicions were confirmed. It was no boy! Rather, a very beautiful woman. The man stared down at Daphne, admiring her beauty. Why, the poor girl was half-dead—already her ghostly pallor was turning to a fevered red flush.

"What are you gawking at? Get busy with my orders, leave us alone!" barked Aristide. The innkeeper bowed his way from the room, nearly knocking down the waiter carrying a tray of brandy.

Aristide cradled Daphne's head in his arms as he pressed the glass of amber liquid to her lips. He had become truly worried about her. Her face was hot with fever and her full lips were dry and parched.

"Drink this, my darling. It will give you strength," he said, forcing a drop of brandy down her throat at last. Daphne took another swallow and coughed.

A delicious sensation of warmth began to creep over Daphne's body as the heat of the fire reached her. Between the fire and the brandy, Daphne felt as though she was being warmed both inside and outside. Warm hands, large and soft, held her small cold hands and chafed them. It was Aristide. Daphne relaxed and allowed him to care for her.

Aristide looked down at Daphne and noted that she seemed to be recovering well from her chill. He smiled. A little food and another glass of wine and she would be his. The light of the fire and the flickering candles in the room made Daphne's hair look like burnished gold. Aristide yearned to touch her, but he restrained himself. Now was not the time. It would only alarm her and warn her.

Daphne ate some bread and milk for dinner and watched in amazement as Aristide consumed an enormous dinner of lamb and roast potatoes, crusty bread, and glass after glass of red wine. After dinner they both drank steaming mugs of coffee in preparation for getting under way again. Daphne dreaded returning to the saddle and the night's cold winds, but if she was to escape from Caleb and find Rene again, she had no choice but to endure her flight. Even now, Caleb could be on her trail. Daphne sighed wearily and stretched her aching muscles. Riding again would be torture.

"I am ready to continue," said Daphne.

"Impossible. Really, my dear, you are too tired. I will not risk your health. We can stay the night here safely and travel on in the morning."

"Oh, no! Caleb may be after us already. We've no time to lose."

"Nonsense, my dear, don't make yourself frantic. You will be just fine. I will protect you from Caleb. I should say, my love, that Caleb is the least of your worries."

Daphne's eyes widened in surprise as Aristide moved closer to her, his coal-black eyes fixed on her face, lustful and intent. He put his arms around her and began to caress her. Daphne struggled against his advances, wriggling to free herself of his embrace. He let her go.

"I see the kitten has claws, but I think we shall find that they will be useless. I am sure that in the end you will enjoy making love to me. You are an experienced woman and I am a man who knows how to give pleasure. Submit to me," he finished, his voice gone suddenly silky and pleading.

"Never," cried Daphne, grasping the wine carafe and desperately striking out at Aristide. The blow landed on his head and Aristide crumpled forward, the wound on the back of his head already bleeding.

Daphne rose in horror, pushing Aristide's unconscious body off her lap and, in so doing, smearing her hands with his blood. She pulled on her cloak, her heart pounding, terrified lest someone come in and find her. Ready to leave, she leaned down toward Aristide, afraid that she had killed him, but afraid also that at any moment he might leap up and attack her again.

I must be sure I haven't killed him, thought Daphne, forcing herself to check whether he was still breathing. She sighed with relief.

"The other gentleman's had a bit too much to

drink," said Daphne to the innkeeper as she mounted her horse. "Put him to bed in a few minutes. I'm going on without him." Before the man could say a word in reply, she spurred her horse and was away.

Chapter 21

Daphne urged her horse on, bringing her riding crop down against its flanks. The mare seemed to spring to life beneath her as she galloped out of the small village and toward Calais. The wind flew past Daphne, stinging rain into her face and catching her hair.

The wind soon began to chill Daphne's bones. Still she pressed on in fear and desperation, terrified that Aristide, as well as Caleb, might overtake her.

The road stretched on endlessly, leading she knew not where. Aristide had been her guide and she did not know the way. Daphne resolved not to worry, but to press forward until she could go no farther.

After a time, the cold winds no longer troubled her. In fact, she felt hot and feverish. Daphne longed to throw off her heavy cloak and let the cooling air reach her burning skin. Soon, as she had expected, chills took over and her teeth chattered violently.

How can I go on? she asked herself. Even the horse is nearly spent. Daphne allowed the animal to slow from a canter to a gentle trot and then slumped forward against her neck to try to get a moment's rest.

The mare became confused when the hands holding her reins relaxed their grip, letting the reins fall against her neck. It felt almost as if she had no rider and yet there was still that weight on her back, grown even heavier perhaps. The horse snorted and ambled down the road trying to smell water or oats. Finding neither, she stood at last by the side of the road, head down, eating grass.

Dawn broke slowly over this isolated bit of French countryside. The first red rays of the sun battled their way through the clouds, sending a shaft of light across the flat, furrowed fields, revealing a group of women in white, bent almost double as they made the ground ready for the first spring planting. Standing up for a moment to wipe the sweat from her brow, one of the women saw the horse and the lifeless form of a rider in the distance by the road.

"Sisters!" she cried. "Look, over there. There is an injured man on that horse." The other women looked up. They approached the horse and rider.

"We'll take them to the convent. Mother will know what to do. The man is feverish, but he is alive," said one, gripping the horse's bridle in a calloused hand and leading her toward the large stone buildings in the distance. Two sisters walked beside the horse, supporting the limp figure.

When they had reached the low stone buildings, the nuns pulled Daphne down from her horse and carried her into the room reserved for visitors. As they did so, they realized that she was a woman and exchanged startled glances.

The Mother Superior allowed Daphne to remain at the convent, for she was too ill to be moved. A sister was assigned to nurse her and to sit beside her day and night.

Life in the convent went on about the unconscious girl. The sisters spoke only when necessary, keeping silent the rest of the day, their lips moving in constant prayer. The only sounds in the convent were of their wooden-soled shoes echoing against the stone walks, their rosary beads clinking softly as they moved about.

For days, Daphne lay without waking, tossing feverishly and losing herself in delirious dreams. Her temperature remained high and although the nuns administered medicines, they had little effect. The sisters feared for her life.

Suddenly one day, Daphne's eyes fluttered open. The world around her swam into view, revealing a narrow room with stone walls, devoid of any furniture or decoration except for a wooden crucifix at the foot of the bed. Daphne shut her eyes again.

When Daphne looked again, she saw a woman's face surrounded by pure white veils. Her lips moved and yet no sound came forth. Daphne continued to stare at the woman in white, wondering who she could be and what she was doing by her bedside. She had no memory of how she had come to this place.

"Where am I?" Daphne asked softly.

The woman's smooth brow creased in a small frown and she hesitated a moment before replying. When she did speak, it was not in English. It took

Daphne a moment to realize that the woman was speaking to her in French.

Daphne repeated her question in French and the woman answered. "You are at the Convent of the Sacred Heart."

Gradually the events of the past months came back to Daphne. She relived the sorrow of losing her child, the escape from Caleb, the flight with Aristide and finally that last dreadful scene in which she had knocked him unconscious. Slowly, Daphne pieced together her flight, the cold night and the fever that had led her to the convent.

"What day is it?"

The nun told her a week had passed since the sisters had found her. Daphne's heart sank as she realized the ship she had intended to take from Calais had long since sailed.

"I must leave now. I am ready to go. Where are my clothes?" asked Daphne frantically.

The sister gently pushed Daphne back against her pillows. "You may not leave until I say that you are well. Those are the Mother Superior's orders. You are not yet well. You have not eaten for a week. That is what we will do now and then we will talk," said the nun with great firmness. "I will go and get your food. Please remain in bed."

The Convent of the Sacred Heart was an ancient and isolated one. The sisters lived a life of quiet contemplation and prayer, supporting themselves by tilling the land around the convent and raising sheep. From her room, Daphne could hear the sisters singing their Latin prayers. She was not allowed into the chapel, for she was only a visitor, but the singing was soothing as it echoed through the old stone halls.

"Sister," said Daphne one day to Angelique, the nun who had been nursing her, "it's so peaceful and lovely here. I wish I could stay forever."

"You could, if you were called, but I think you have not been. Your duty lies elsewhere."

"Were you called? What does that mean?" Angelique did not reply. "It sounds so exciting. When I was a child, I used to imagine going to Africa to do missionary work. It would have been so thrilling."

Daphne and Angelique continued their walk in the convent's orchard, their clothes swirling about them. From a distance, they looked like two nuns. Angelique wore the long, white habit of a sister who has taken her full vows, complete with its starched head dress that made a small triangle of her face. Daphne wore the simple grey dress of the novice. It was made of thick wool, taken from the convent's own flocks and woven by the sisters.

"Soon I will be leaving and going back into the world. All that seems so far away, but I know that once I am there again, these weeks in the convent will seem like a dream.

"Oh, Sister, I feel that I have been healed in more than body. And I owe you and the other sisters so much."

Angelique replied, "Now we must go in. Mother Mary Augustine wishes to speak to you. It is time for you to leave us. Come." Together, they walked back to the convent and Sister Angelique led Daphne into the Mother Superior's office and left her there.

"Be calm, my child," soothed Mother Mary Augustine, motioning to Daphne to be seated. "I know that you are apprehensive. You wonder where you will go next and what will become of you. The sisters and I want only to help you. You are well now and ready to leave us. May I ask you where you want to go?"

"I was on my way to America when I fell ill. I'd like to resume my journey. I think I have enough money to buy passage on a ship. Sister Angelique said that you were holding it for me."

"Yes, your money is here when you need it. You must not act rashly, my child. News has reached us that there are many people who are trying to find you. I don't think that they wish you well and so we have not told them that you are with us." Daphne began to speak. The Mother Superior held up a hand to silence her. "There is no need to explain. Those matters are of the world. You will go back to America, but you need our help. We've decided that you'll wear the habit of a lay sister and that Sister Mary Chrisanta will accompany you as far as Calais. You should be safe once you are on board ship. Is that agreeable to you?"

"Oh, yes," answered Daphne. "Thank you so much for your kindness."

Angelique awakened Daphne at dawn the next morning and dressed her in the habit of a lay sister. It was made of the same grey material as the novice's habit. Angelique swathed Daphne's head in white linen, covering her red-blonde hair. Over the linen, she placed a short grey veil.

Angelique giggled mischievously as she examined Daphne in her habit. "You look very different than you did when you first came here disguised as a boy.

Yes, you make a very proper looking nun now. Ah, I shall miss you. Well, off you go. I will remember you in my prayers."

Angelique kissed Daphne's cheek and pushed her toward the door as Sister Mary Christanta knocked.

Daphne opened her mouth to speak, but Angelique shook her head, indicating that she keep silent. There was nothing more for them to say to one another. Their two worlds were taking them apart now, and that was how it should be.

The coach took two days to reach Calais. Daphne and Sister Mary Chrisanta rode in silence, speaking neither to one another nor to their fellow passengers. Sister Mary Chrisanta was a dour woman who had spent fifty years in the convent, having entered it at the age of thirteen. Her worn hands busied themselves with her rosary beads as the coach jolted toward Calais. Daphne marveled at her concentration. If any prayers reached God, surely those single-minded petitions of Sister Mary Chrisanta must be among them, thought Daphne.

Once at Calais, Sister Mary Chrisanta accompanied Daphne like a silent shadow. Together, they booked Daphne's passage on a ship leaving for New York the next day, went to the telegraph office to send a message to Lilleth in Pittsburgh and then found a local convent where they were to spend the night.

The clerk in the telegraph office spent a long time wondering over the message the nun with the American accent had left him.

"Arriving New York June 25. Tell Rene I love him."

Chapter 22

Chapter 72

Daphne's second voyage across the Atlantic was quite different from her first. On her trip to France, she had been in a first-class stateroom, a young girl accompanied by her maid. Returning to New York, she occupied a tiny chamber in the second-class section of the ship, which she shared with three spinster sisters from Concord, Massachusetts.

The passage was a smooth one and Daphne found that time hung heavily on her hands. She was exhausted from her ordeals and saddened by leaving Isabel and Nana. Dressed as a nun, she could not lie about on deck chairs reading novels like the rest of the passengers. Such behavior would have been highly improper. Daphne had to content herself by taking long walks on deck, enjoying the feel of the wind and spray of the ocean against her face, gathering her strength.

Daphne had rather enjoyed playing at being a nun for the first few days of the voyage, but now she was tired of it. There was nothing for her to do. Yes, life on board the ship was very dull.

In the first-class salon of the *Albion*, life was far from dull. Caleb Winters relaxed, smoking an after-dinner cigar and wondering idly whether he should join Colonel Whitman's baccarat game or attend the captain's ball. He stretched and yawned. The sea air made one so damned sleepy.

Frivolous thoughts of what to do with his evening did not long occupy Caleb's mind, however. Soon, he returned again to the problem of Daphne Slater. Her disappearance still mystified him. She had rushed out of the chapel and been gone before he could catch her. Vanished into thin air. But of course, she had not. It had been a simple enough matter for Caleb to find the cab driver who had picked her up. The man had remembered Daphne quite clearly and had, for a rather large sum, told Caleb where he had taken her. The woman, Nana, was less cooperative, but Caleb soon realized that she was not harboring Daphne any longer.

Caleb's last few days in Paris had been spent in a fruitless search for Daphne. He had returned to Nana's house in the Rue Mouffetard and questioned her. He had wanted to learn the name of the person who had accompanied Daphne on her flight from Paris, but Nana steadfastly had refused to tell him anything.

Isabel was afraid for Daphne, and worried about her niece taking a long voyage alone. She refused to see Caleb at all and contented herself with writing long letters to her brother and sister in Pittsburgh, excoriating Caleb's behavior. She was careful not to inform them that Daphne had left Paris.

She also painted a beautiful portrait of Daphne as the dead Ophelia floating down a stream, a peaceful expression on her face, her garments billowing about her and flowers in her hair. The painting was one of the best she had ever done, for Isabel had poured her sorrow at the loss of her niece into it, as well as her fears for Daphne's unmapped future with the fugitive Rene.

Caleb felt sure that Daphne would try to return to America and to Rene. If she was still in France, he believed she would be on her way to a port. Calais was the nearest port to Paris, so Caleb, having completed his investigations there, took the road to Calais and began the tedious job of asking in inns and coaching stations for news of Daphne.

Eventually, his persistence paid off and he found the inn at which Daphne and Aristide had stopped. The innkeeper, over a glass of wine and with a small sum to help his memory, was only too happy to tell Caleb what had taken place in his inn.

Caleb was at first surprised that Daphne should have had the strength and determination to defend herself so violently against de la Tour, but then he smiled to himself. "That girl certainly has a lot of spirit. I still remember that day on Lookout Point when she kicked me in the shins like a wild thing and then jumped onto her horse and rode off like an Indian."

No one else in the area had seen the slim girl in boys' clothing. Even her horse had disappeared. Caleb was puzzled. How could her trail just have vanished? Someone in the area must know where she was. She couldn't have gotten far, ill and traveling alone.

Caleb waited in the lavishly decorated foyer of Aristide de la Tour's Paris townhouse. He shifted his weight angrily on the ornately carved black bench on which he was seated.

Really, Caleb thought, to be kept waiting like a tradesman while some French fool decides if he'll see me. Daphne will pay for all the trouble she's caused me when I find her!

Finally, a liveried footman ushered Caleb into an even more ornately decorated drawing room. Crystal chandeliers hung from the gilded ceiling, paintings by the finest French artists looked disdainfully down from the walls. The furniture was delicate, standing on spindly gold legs, draped in the palest blue brocade. The color of the cushions reminded Caleb of Catherine. That was just the color of the dress she had worn on the night of Jeb Slater's party.

A door opened behind him, interrupting his inspection of the room and its decorations. Caleb took in Aristide de la Tour in one appraising glance. He was displeased with what he saw. The man was obviously distinguished and well bred, but too much of the idler for Caleb's taste. Caleb was certain that he had never been inside a factory in his life, never known what it was to go down in a coal mine. Life for this rich aristocrat was merely a game. He was not a man that Caleb could respect.

Aristide returned Caleb's gaze. He was familiar with Caleb's type. He had met many such men while he was in America. They were concerned only with business and thought of everything in terms of profit and loss. Their businesses were their very souls, money was their lifeblood. As a student of humanity, Aristide found such men moderately interesting, but otherwise he found them intolerable. Aristide wondered why this man had come to visit him. It could hardly, for a man of his sort, be a purely social call.

Caleb broke the spell that had taken hold of them. "I believe you may be able to assist me. To be blunt, where is Daphne Slater?"

Aristide started. He hoped that he would not have to fight a duel with this man over the girl. That would all be so tiresome. If he won he would have to leave France once again, and if he lost. . . .

"I am sorry to say that I do not know. Miss Slater got away from me. Now I recall your name. Your Christian name is Caleb, is it not?" Caleb nodded. "When I last saw her, she was running away from you. Then she ran away from me as well. A most elusive creature."

"I find that flippant tone of yours offensive. This is a serious matter. The police are involved," said Caleb, his eyes blazing indignantly.

"I am most sorry to be unable to assist you. I, too, would like to know where she has gone. I made certain inquiries when I regained consciousness. You know that she hit me over the head with a wine carafe? As I was saying, these inquiries proved fruitless. The innkeeper saw her riding off into the night and that is the last that has been seen of her. But, I am sure that you know all that already."

"Yes, I do, but I thought you might have found her and be harboring her."

"Not at all, my good man. The lady is not here."

Caleb believed the man. "Do you have any idea where she might be?"

"On her way to America, to rejoin her prince charming." Aristide shrugged. "In my opinion, that one is too much trouble. Dangerous, in fact," he remarked, rubbing his head.

"I'll draw my own conclusions on that score, thank you." With those words, Caleb turned on his heel and left the room.

Caleb returned to the small village where Daphne had last been seen, but once again, his search was fruitless. He passed the forbidding walls of the Convent of the Sacred Heart many times, but only once thought that Daphne might be within. The peasants, however, assured him that the nuns allowed no visitors. They were shut off from all society, they said, and did not even allow visits from their own families. Caleb shuddered at the finality of their destiny.

Caleb had finally begun to realize that he was wasting his time searching for Daphne. Neither Nana nor Isabel would tell him anything at all. Pressing business in Pittsburgh demanded his attention and he was loath to leave Jeb in charge for any longer than was absolutely necessary. Besides, Caleb had a score to settle with Jeb, and if he couldn't get his hands on Daphne, there was still her father . . .

Dance music from the ballroom broke into Caleb's thoughts and he stood up from the table, putting out his cigar. He would go into the ballroom and squire the silly but amiable girls around. He sighed. They were all nothing compared to the beautiful Daphne.

On the deck below, Daphne's feet tapped in time

to the music that floated down from the ballroom. She looked out across the ocean at the path the moon was taking and wondered what Rene was doing at that very moment.

Rene was living in a tenement in New York, trying to earn money for his passage to Paris. He was anxious to join Daphne and make a new life for themselves far away from all their troubles. Work in the coal mines and the unions was closed to him, and his escape from prison had been all the luck he could count on for a while. He wanted to go west to Santa Fe, where he had heard that a man could make an honest living without people prying into his life. Daphne would have enough pluck to enter wholeheartedly into such a life. What a splendid girl she was, he thought, and how he loved her.

Lilleth's visit to his cramped quarters on Hester Street came as a great surprise to Rene. He had feared he would never see his dear friend again. "Lilleth!" he greeted. "Have you any news of Daphne? It's not bad, is it?"

"No, no, it's not bad, Rene," said Lilleth, taking both of his hands. "Your struggles are over. Daphne will soon be home. She wired me the other day, and as I had to be in New York to attend some meetings, I thought I would come and tell you in person. I'm so happy for you both."

The two old friends went out to a small Italian restaurant and had a lovely evening. They talked excitedly about Daphne's homecoming. Then they turned to talk of the settlement house and of Pittsburgh. Rene still missed it all very much and was torn by the awful realization that, as a fugitive from justice, he could never go back to his home town and could never help Lilleth at the settlement house again. It was all so unfair and it made him furious.

"I'm sorry, too, Rene, but it's impossible. Forget the past. You and Daphne have no future in Pittsburgh. There would be too many memories for both of you, and no one would forget that Daphne is the daughter of one of the richest men in town. The gossip about you never would cease.

"You've done your share for us in Pittsburgh. There will be other important things for you to do in Santa Fe. Your destiny lies out there. Embrace it." There was more fire than usual in Lilleth's eyes, and she spoke as though it was her life they were discussing.

"Lilleth . . . ," Rene began hesitantly. He did not know how to ask her why she cared so deeply. "You've been so wonderful to Daphne and me. It's almost as though you knew just what we were going through."

"I do," she answered softly. Rene's eyes urged her to explain. "I . . . I," she stopped. "It's still so terrible, even after all these years." She laughed softly. "Even we old maids have our secret sorrows."

Rene took her hand across the table and squeezed it, surprised at her sudden revelation. In all the time he had known Lilleth, she never had hinted at any personal life at all. He wondered what had happened, but knew he would never find out. Lilleth was reticent with even her closest friends.

"Tell Daphne I'm sorry I missed her." Lilleth smiled as she and Rene parted. "I hope we'll all meet again in happier times. I can't imagine myself going West, though, I must say!"

*　　*　　*

Daphne continued staring out over the sea at the moon, gently tapping her foot to the music. Rene filled her mind. How could she find him? If Lilleth didn't know where he was, she would have a long search ahead of her. Deep in her heart, Daphne expected Rene to be waiting for her as she stepped off the gangplank in New York, though she knew how foolish that was. She imagined him whisking her off to Santa Fe, stopping only to marry. Daphne sighed. Rene was still so far away. Would their dreams ever come true?

Chapter 23

Daphne was on deck very early on the morning the *Albion* was to dock in New York harbor. She had been too nervous to sleep that night. To think that Rene might even be in New York! As she lay in her berth sleepless with anticipation, Rene might be lying in bed in New York thinking of her. Daphne tried to be stern with herself and prepare herself for the disappointment she would feel when Rene did not meet the ship. There was no chance at all that he would do so. Why, he was probably not in New York at all. It is foolish to think that Lilleth can have reached him in time, she admonished herself.

Slowly the sky began to lighten. Daphne leapt up and began to dress, trying to be quiet enough not to wake the other women in the cabin. She donned her nun's disguise for what she hoped would be the last time, carefully wrapping her hair in the pure white linen and draping the veil over it. Daphne sighed as she did so, thinking of Sister Angelique and

295

the Mother Superior. The quiet, peaceful ways of the convent belonged to another world.

Once on deck, Daphne's soul felt more quiet and more at peace. Out in the open air, away from the clammy darkness of the cabin, Daphne could breathe freely. With each throb of the ship's massive engine, the *Albion* moved closer to New York, and her face shone with joy as she caught sight of her native land on the horizon. Rene! was the thought that filled her mind and thrilled Daphne.

As the sky lightened, losing the white tint of early dawn at sea, red clouds streaked across it and the sun appeared as a giant fireball. The dawn breeze blew gently, ruffling the folds of Daphne's habit and playing with her veil. A wonderful feeling of well-being took hold of Daphne, assuring her that nothing could go wrong on this day, that finally, the wretched destiny that had dogged her and Rene and kept them apart was over. Daphne smiled, hungrily scanning the distant horizon.

Daphne went inside for breakfast. Everyone she spoke to seemed so lovable. She overflowed with happiness and longed to share that happiness with everyone. Even the coffee and stale rolls seemed the finest food on earth. And the grumpy spinsters from Concord took on a new, friendly appeal.

Once again on deck, Daphne was pleased to see that the ship sailed even closer to port. The sight of the city in the distance sent a thrill through Daphne. To think, as she watched the land draw nearer, that she was seeing the buildings coming into focus! Daphne willed the *Albion* to move faster.

It seemed to Daphne that the boat would never reach the shore. The hands of her watch crept around the dial and more than once Daphne held it to her ear thinking that it had stopped. She was afire with impatience to reach shore and see if Rene had come to meet her as she so fervently hoped he would.

At last the boat approached the pier and the sailors threw their heavy lines down to the men waiting on the dock. Daphne's heart sang with joy. She was even more impatient to leave the boat than ever, but still the gangplank had not been laid down. Daphne's hands clutched the ship's rail as she waited for the gangplank to be lowered.

After an eternity of waiting, Daphne was assisted down the gangplank by one of the sailors. Her small valise was handed to her and she was left standing in the crowd. After several minutes of being buffeted about by the crowd, Daphne felt ready to give up her search for Rene. It was fruitless, she felt sure. All about her were happy family groups, reunited after long absences. How she envied them!

With a heavy heart, she made her way through the crowd to the street. There was little point in waiting around by the pier. Daphne made up her mind to face the truth. Rene had been unable to come. The painful truth weighed upon her mind, crowding out all other thoughts.

Suddenly, Daphne stood still, realizing she had nowhere to go. The crowd eddied about her, people pushing her and cursing under their breath. She was blocking the way. How stupid she had been not to make plans. Daphne knew only one address in New York, that of the hotel she and Letty had stayed in the night before her ship sailed for France. She supposed she would have to go there.

Daphne lifted her valise again and walked resolutely toward the hackney cabs, hoping that she would be able to get one without too much waiting.

Daphne uttered an exclamation of annoyance when she saw the long line of people waiting for cabs. Nothing was going right. The feeling of happiness and joy that she had had as the ship drew closer to land evaporated, leaving a bitter residue. Daphne began to walk toward the end of the line, resigning herself to a long wait.

"Sister!" a voice called. "Sure and there's always room for one o' the nuns in my cab," cried one of the drivers in a thick Irish brogue.

Daphne smiled at him. "Oh, I couldn't take someone else's place," she said, approaching the man.

"It's no trouble at all, I'm telling you. Haven't I already got meself another passenger? You wouldn't be minding traveling with a gentleman, now would ye?"

Daphne shook her head and allowed the man to help her into the carriage. In a flash he had climbed up onto his seat and the carriage was moving away from the docks at a smart pace.

Daphne's heart gave a sickening lurch when she saw the man sitting beside her. The smile vanished from her face and she struggled to fight down an urge to throw herself from the moving carriage. Caleb Winters sat beside her!

Daphne quickly put her head down and pulled her veil forward to cover her face. She folded her hands meekly in her lap and stared intently at them. Perhaps Caleb had not seen her face. Perhaps he would not recognize her disguised as a nun. Daphne could feel him beside her like a dangerous animal, crouched, ready to attack. She was sure that he knew who she was and was only torturing her by pretending not to. Her lips were dry and her throat tightened with anxiety. It seemed as though she had been in the carriage with him for hours and yet only a few seconds had passed. She did not know how she would endure the rest of the ride and yet she knew that she had to. There was no way out.

The presence of the nun vexed Caleb. He had hired the carriage and expected to be alone in it, and now suddenly this nun was thrust upon him. Really, he thought, hackney drivers took insufferable liberties these days. Caleb decided to ignore the woman, but there was something about her that wouldn't let him. Something familiar about her face. Of course, he had only glimpsed it for a moment before she had pulled her veil forward, cutting off his view. She had been deliberately trying to prevent him from seeing her face, but why? Caleb shrugged. Perhaps she was merely modest and disliked being so close to a man. Caleb tried to put the matter out of his mind, but that glimpse of her face kept floating just out of his reach, like some tantalizing puzzle.

"Daphne!" he cried aloud, striking his knee with his fist.

The startled face of the nun turned around, her eyes wide with fear. It was Daphne. They stared at one another for a moment without speaking.

"So," gloated Caleb when he could speak at last, "fate has brought us together. You thought you could escape from me, but you see, you cannot. We are destined to be together, Daphne. You cannot escape me."

Daphne opened her lips to speak, but no sound came forth. This could not really be happening. She had run from him so many times, and so many times he had caught her. She was tired of running. Rene was gone. Why go on fighting? Why not accept her fate? Perhaps Caleb was right. Perhaps it was her destiny to be with him. She did not even know where Rene was. She felt that every ounce of will had been drained from her, leaving her without the strength to fight Caleb any longer. She felt nothing and allowed the movement of the carriage to capture her full attention.

Suddenly the carriage halted, throwing both Daphne and Caleb forward. The sudden movement shocked Daphne into action and she wrenched open the door of the carriage and leapt out, flinging her valise against Caleb, fending him off while she slammed the door shut.

Daphne stumbled forward onto the street, nearly tripping on the long skirts of her habit. She began to run, hearing Caleb's bellow of rage and pain. The carriage door had shut on his hand.

The streets were crowded with carriages and carts. A streetcar was stopped in the middle of the street. All the drivers were yelling at once, ordering the others to move on and swearing at the top of their lungs. The driver of the cab Daphne had been in had not even noticed her precipitous exit, for he was too busy quarreling with the other drivers.

Daphne stood for half a second, staring in bewilderment about her. Where could she run? The streets seemed too crowded with people to allow escape. There was, Daphne knew, no time for thought. Caleb already was jumping from the carriage, vowing to kill her and cursing about his injured hand. Blindly she ran forward, weaving in and out of traffic, trying to avoid being stepped on by the heavy dray horses stamping their huge hooves.

Passers-by looked on with interest at the headlong flight of the young nun. Why, they wondered, was she running? Why was the well-dressed, tall blond man running after her? But no one did anything to stop either of them. They'd all seen stranger sights.

One of the passengers on the streetcar looked on the scene with particular interest. He was new to New York, and so did not look upon a gentleman in fine clothes chasing a beautiful young nun through the streets as an everyday affair. Also, though he could not see her face, there was something familiar about the woman. Suddenly he realized that it was not the nun he knew, but the man chasing her. He owed that one a bad turn if ever he owed anyone. He jumped up. Jamming his hat firmly down on his head and pushing people aside, he leapt from the streetcar, chasing Caleb Winters, fury rising with every footstep.

In the narrow alley, Daphne's footsteps rang out as her heavy shoes hit the paving stones. Daphne could almost feel Caleb's breath against the back of her neck. She tried to continue running, but suddenly she felt as though she couldn't move another step. Exhaustion overtook her and she found herself slowing down.

She turned her head. Caleb was so close that his outstretched hand was nearly touching her. On his face was a look of pure loathing. Daphne gasped at the force of his hatred.

Just as Caleb's hand gripped her shoulder, pulling her toward him, Daphne heard other footsteps.

Caleb heard them too and turned to see, still keeping a firm hold on Daphne.

"Let her go!" cried the man.

Caleb uttered a cry of rage and yelled, "Mind your own business. She's mine to do with as I please."

Just then the intruder balled his fist and threw a punch at Caleb, sending him reeling backward. Daphne had pulled herself free of Caleb and she now moved farther away, safely out of range.

She stared at the man who had come to her rescue. But it couldn't be. Like something in a dream, the man was Rene! As yet he had not recognized her, so intent was he on his struggle with Caleb. Daphne's heart skipped a beat as she saw Caleb rise and fix his hate-filled glare at Rene. Their eyes looked murder at one another.

"So it's you!" cried Caleb, at last. "Up to mischief again. This time you won't get away so easily.".

The two men circled one another warily, keeping their distance, but looking for an opportunity to strike.

"Yes, it is I. You had best beware."

Caleb's laugh rang out in the narrow alley. "I have nothing to fear from you, you coward."

Rene's grey eyes blazed hatred as he hit Caleb again and again. Daphne stood watching them, too frightened to move, but not wishing to distract Rene. She drew back into the shadows of a doorway, making herself as small as possible. The two men took no notice of her, so intent were they on their struggle. Daphne bit her lip to keep from crying out, as Caleb advanced on Rene and struck him a powerful blow to the stomach. Rene doubled over in pain. With great effort, he forced himself to straighten up, just in time, for Caleb was upon him quickly.

Rene struck out blindly against Caleb. He put all his strength and his memories of the prison Caleb had sent him to behind each punch.

Caleb continued to pommel Rene savagely, seeing in Rene his adversary in love and his enemy at work. His head spun with the punches Rene had landed, and he began to weaken.

The two men made a striking contrast, Caleb's gold hair gleaming in the sun, his finely tailored jacket ripped at the shoulders, and Rene, dark-haired, his body hard and streamlined from a lifetime spent laboring. Blood dripped from a cut over Caleb's eye, soaking his fine white silk shirt and bathing the left side of his face. Rene used the blood as a target and hit there again and again.

Both men wondered briefly how it was possible to go on fighting and yet each continued to fight, driven by hatred. Then Caleb began to feel his strength ebbing from him. All he could do was remain standing and try to defend himself from Rene's blows. He kept his hands up, forcing himself to assume the correct boxing stance. But somehow, he already felt beaten. He would not stand for that feeling and his pride forced him to launch one final attack.

Rene had been expecting him to do just that and he was ready. He seemed to know exactly where Caleb would throw his punches and he parried them expertly. At last, Caleb's strength was spent. He had exhausted himself with this last barrage of blows that weren't able to find their mark. Rene saw him weakening, noting the way he swayed on his feet as though his legs were not strong enough to support

him. With one final surge of power, Rene took aim
and swung at Caleb's jaw. Caleb tottered for a moment and then fell over backward, no longer conscious.

Rene stood completely still, utterly exhausted. He
looked down at Caleb and felt incredibly relieved to
see that the man was still alive. Rene shook his head
to clear it. Above the loud rushing noise in his ears
came a voice calling his name. He shook his head
again. That voice belonged to someone so dear that
he must not even believe that he was hearing it. She
might not even have reached America yet, and if she
had, how would he find her?

A slender hand tugged at his sleeve. Rene looked
down at those delicate fingers in disbelief.

"Rene?" Daphne whispered.

Rene turned to see the vision that had haunted
him all these months looking earnestly up at him, her
beautiful blue eyes swimming with tears. It was the
young nun Caleb had been chasing. Daphne!

"Don't you recognize me? It's me, Daphne," she
said softly. "Please, say something to me, Rene."

"Is it really you?" Rene reached out his hand as
though to touch her, but then drew it away as though
he'd been burned.

"What is it, Rene? It is I, Daphne. Oh, my darling, how I love you."

"But, but. . . ." stammered Rene. "How is it possible? You're a nun."

"No, no," cried Daphne, laughing with relief now
that she knew Rene had recognized her and understood what was troubling him. "I am not a nun."

Rene looked at her in disbelief. What incredible

nonsense was this? Anyone could see that she was a nun.

Daphne pulled the veil impatiently from her head and tugged at the linen wrappings that covered her hair. Rene watched in astonishment as she freed her red-blonde hair and shook it out about her.

"It was only a disguise! I haven't become a nun. I've come back to marry you, if you'll still have me."

"Daphne," cried Rene, sweeping her into his arms and holding her as tightly to him as he dared. "I can't believe it. It's really you! I'll never, never let you go again. We're together at last!"

"Yes," Daphne sobbed. "At last!"

ROMANCE LOVERS DELIGHT

Purchase any first book at regular price of $4.95 & choose any second book for $2.95 plus $1.50 shipping & handling for each book.

_____**LOVE'S SECRET JOURNEY** by Margaret Hunter. She found a man of mystery in an ancient land.

_____**DISTANT THUNDER** by Karen A. Bale. While sheltering a burning love she fights for her honor.

_____**DESTINY'S THUNDER** by Elizabeth Bright. She risks her life for her passionate captain.

_____**DIAMOND OF DESIRE** by Candice Adams. On the eve of a fateful war she meets her true love.

_____**A HERITAGE OF PASSION** by Elizabeth Bright. A wild beauty matches desires with a dangerous man.

_____**SHINING NIGHTS** by Linda Trent. A handsome stranger, mystery & intrigue at Queen's table.

_____**DESIRE'S LEGACY** by Elizabeth Bright. An unforgotten love amidst a war torn land.

_____**THE BRAVE & THE LONELY** by R. Vaughn. Five families, their loves and passion against a war.

_____**SHADOW OF LOVE** by Ivy St. David. Wealthy mine owner lost her love.

_____**A LASTING SPLENDOR** by Elizabeth Bright. Imperial Beauty struggles to forget her amorous affairs.

_____**ISLAND PROMISE** by W. Ware Lynch. Heiress escapes life of prostitution to find her island lover.

_____**A BREATH OF PARADISE** by Carol Norris. Bronzed Fiji Island lover creates turbulent sea of love.

_____**RUM COLONY** by Terry Nelson Bonner. Wild untamed woman bent on a passion for destructive love.

_____**A SOUTHERN WIND** by Gene Lancour. Secret family passions bent on destruction.

_____**CHINA CLIPPER** by John Van Zwienen. Story of sailing ships beautiful woman tantalizing love.

_____**A DESTINY OF LOVE** by Ivy St. David. A coal miners daughter's desires and romantic dreams.